A PERFECTLY (UN)TIMELY PROPOSAL

A PRIDE & PREJUDICE VARIATION

JENNIFER JOY

A Perfectly (Un)timely Proposal: A Pride & Prejudice Variation
Love's Little Helpers, Book 2

Published by Jennifer Joy

Email: contact@jenniferjoywrites.com

ISBN-13: 978-1-944795-44-3

CONTENTS

FREE BOOK

Want a free novelette?
Join Jennifer Joy's newsletter!

CHAPTER 1

APRIL 9, 1812~ROSINGS PARK, KENT

Fitzwilliam Darcy cleared his throat and regarded his reflection in the mirror. Lifting his chin, his posture exuding supreme confidence (but which had maddeningly failed to mollify his nerves since his arrival at Rosings), he practiced once again. "I trust your family is in good health?"

He frowned at the waver in his tone. That would not do. Shaking his hands and stretching his neck from side to side, he forced his shoulders down and attempted a smile. "The weather has been favorable for walking."

Darcy grimaced at the popinjay looking back at him. Chalmers had tied his cravat in a fussy, frillish waterfall of folds Darcy had never before consented to, his own taste being more restrained than that of the dandies of the ton… or, as it would seem, his own valet.

His cravat, however, was the least of Darcy's difficulties. Trivial talk had always been difficult for him, but Miss Elizabeth expected it of him. She had told him to practice.

So here he was, standing in front of the looking glass in the middle of his room in his best attire, combed and coaxed into the latest fashion, talking to himself. He was a fool.

Shaking his hands again, he wiped his sweaty palms against his brushed breeches and tried once more to relax when his stomach was tied in knots and his tongue tasted of bilious acid. Taking a deep breath, he smiled, but his increasing nerves either made the expression too large or too small. This misery was unbearable.

Chalmers slipped inside the room. "The Collinses have arrived."

Darcy inhaled sharply. This was the moment he had anticipated and dreaded since he had made his decision. He pulled out the ruby pin holding his cravat in place, pretending not to see Chalmers' disappointment. "A simple knot will do." Darcy could not propose to the woman he loved resembling a fop… regardless of his valet's droopy eyes and audible sighs.

Miss Elizabeth was the only woman with whom Darcy could imagine spending the rest of his life. He had gone over and over all the objections. They were the same obstacles he had enumerated to his friend Bingley—the very challenges which had ultimately convinced Bingley to separate himself from Miss Elizabeth's eldest sister while proving to Darcy the ardor of his own affection.

He could never abandon Elizabeth as Bingley had Miss Bennet. Then again, Elizabeth was not indifferent to him as Miss Bennet was to Bingley. Such fire in her eyes! Such passion in her speech! Theirs would be a lively union replete with stimulating debates, provocative conversation and, Darcy hoped, hot-blooded affection. He loved Elizabeth. Not even her atrocious family, low station, and lack of connections or dowry could dissuade his heart. He had to have her at his side.

She was the one.

Nodding appreciatively to the offended Chalmers, Darcy swiped a rebellious lock of hair off his forehead, willing the defiant curls to stay in place or at least have the grace not to sprout out from his head. After one final glance at his reflection, he clasped his hands with determination and stepped to the armoire where his brushed coat hung.

Chalmers raised his hand. "They have arrived," he repeated, the next words coming apologetically, "... without Miss Bennet."

It took a moment for understanding to halt Darcy's step. "Miss Elizabeth is not here?"

"Evidently she remained at the parsonage, sir." Chalmers' voice was heavy with regret.

"Why could you not tell me sooner?"

"You asked me to attend to your cravat."

And a man could not speak while tying a knot? Darcy was fairly certain Chalmers knew his mind well enough to read his thought. Proving the depth of his insight, his man pinched his lips and arched his brow. As he could not know how grievously this news altered his employer's plans, Darcy chose to forgive him.

The master of Pemberley had been practicing all day, working himself into a mass of nerves he had never experienced before and wished never to feel again. The only way to dispel his anxiety was to ask the question he had repeated in every mirror and window pane he passed in his aunt's house. How could he woo a lady who was not present?

"Apparently Miss Elizabeth is unwell."

Disappointment warred with concern for his intended. "I hope it is nothing serious?"

Chalmers leaned in—loyal eavesdropping spy that he was. "The maid informed me that Mrs. Collins mentioned a headache."

The breath whooshed out of Darcy's lungs. A headache was a minor ailment, easily provoked (above five minutes in Mr. Collins' or his aunt's company had the same effect on him) and just as easily cured (by removing himself from said pain-producing company). Miss Elizabeth was clever to so smoothly avoid them. Darcy was tempted to claim illness too. The prospect of enduring the next few hours at his aunt's table without the relief of Elizabeth's presence was enough to initiate a dull pounding at the base of his skull. "Thank you, Chalmers."

His valet of over a decade nodded, the crinkle at the edge of his eyes the only sign of pleasure as he helped him into his best coat—the same color of the gown Elizabeth had worn at the Meryton Assembly the day they had first met.

Did she think upon that evening as often as he did? He had been in a boorish mood worsened by the villagers' vulgar talk of his wealth and the ladies shoved before him for inspection like mares at Tattersalls—except Elizabeth. He had thought she avoided him, laughing and dancing and sparing him nary so much as a glance... until he caught her eye as he departed. He had never experienced so much sentiment in one look. It had been the beginning of the end for him. And now, he would have to endure another evening without her company.

Disinclined to join the party in his aunt's drawing room a moment before necessary, Darcy went to Richard's rooms. His cousin's batman was brushing off the shoulders of his coat, so neither turned when Darcy entered.

"Miss Bennet is ill with a headache," Darcy announced, leaning against the wall opposite Richard.

"Really?" Richard's eyebrows popped up. "She seemed well earlier."

Darcy nudged away from the papered partition and

crossed his arms. "You called on her?" Why would Richard call at the parsonage without him?

"Do not get in a huff, Darcy. I chanced across Miss Bennet's path during my walk over the park. We had a lively conversation which ended on a pleasant note when I deposited her safely at the door of the parsonage."

Darcy scowled. He regretted the afternoon wasted with Aunt Catherine's steward. The poor man had no power to effect any of the changes Darcy suggested because his stubborn aunt insisted on doing everything her own way.

Richard rolled his eyes. "Have you gone to the kennels today? Mansell has more puppies than he knows what to do with. Ten Great Danes in one litter and big enough now to get into mischief."

The mere mention of the loathsome breed made Darcy break into a cold sweat.

Richard yammered on. "Only two months old and already the biggest weighs in at thirty pounds! If I had a property of my own, I would be tempted to take one home. Mansell would be grateful. The gamekeeper has been breathing down his neck to cull out the litter. Aunt already has enough to check the wild boar population. Keeping all of them seems excessive."

Darcy had no desire to talk about the kennel keeper's devils when his thoughts were across the lawn at the Hunsford parsonage with Elizabeth.

Richard looked suggestively at Darcy. "You know, Pemberley is large—"

"Absolutely not!" Darcy snapped.

"Come on, Darce. A Great Dane!"

"There is nothing great about them."

Richard narrowed his eyes and grinned. "You are not still afraid—"

"No." Darcy's tone brooked no argument, although his heart raced as though it were attempting to outrun a snarling pack of the vile, mangy curs.

"It is hardly fair for you to allow one minor incident to ruin your opinion of the noble breed."

"They are vicious savages, and I will not allow them on Pemberley property."

Richard shook his head and clucked like a chicken. "You hold a grudge on an entire race because of the poor reaction of one dog?"

"It ran me down and tore into me."

"You exaggerate."

"You did not feel its teeth."

Richard shrugged. "You were in his territory. You should have known better."

Darcy glared at his cousin, the pounding in his skull spreading down his neck and knotting in his shoulders. There was more to the story than that, and Richard knew it. "It was a tenant's home on Pemberley land. I had every right to be where I was."

"You expect the dog to know the distinction? Really,

Darcy, with such high expectations, it is a wonder you have any friends at all."

Gritting his teeth and rubbing his temples, Darcy seethed, "He tore into my… flesh." He observed the grin creeping up Richard's face and knew he had swallowed his cousin's bait. Blast the infernal man.

"And you still have the scar, I presume, to prove it!" Richard guffawed like a ninnyhammer. "Pray do not show me, I beg you."

As if Darcy would.

"Perhaps I shall mention the incident at dinner. See how Mr. Collins pontificates on the merits of turning the other cheek."

Darcy refused to listen to another word. He now had a genuine, full-blown headache of his own. Speaking through clenched teeth, he said, "I am going for a walk."

"Come, Darcy, you take yourself too seriously. You have been anxious lately, and I only meant to lighten your mood."

Darcy crossed the room to the sound of his cousin's endless chatter.

"The hour is late. It is dark. Dinner awaits."

Ignoring him, Darcy opened the door.

More urgently, Richard called after him. "Aunt Catherine shall be cross."

Darcy spun around with a sigh. "Better at me than at you."

He left Richard grumbling in his bedchamber, the

satisfaction Darcy took in turning the table on his cousin lessening the ache in his head. His relief, however, was temporary. Once out of doors, the calm night he had hoped for was marred with throaty barks and shouts.

Darcy looked down the gentle slope at the side of his aunt's formidable abode in the direction of the kennels, his heart jumping into his throat at every shadow. He reminded himself that the snarling overgrown beasts were kept in the kennel and supervised by a capable man who had not once, over the years, had one of his keeps escape during Darcy's visits.

Walking across the lawn away from the noise, Darcy took several deep breaths. It was only when he reached the lane at the edge of the park and spotted one window glowing like a beacon summoning him to Mr. Collins' cottage that he realized what he must do.

He would continue as he had planned. He would walk to the parsonage and ask Elizabeth for her hand in marriage. The decision filled Darcy with resolve, and it was with a firm step and a single-minded heart that he passed through the garden gate and rang the bell.

He breezed by the maid to find Elizabeth sitting with a candle at the table, a pile of letters clutched in her hands.

She startled when she saw him.

He doffed his hat, feeling like a dolt for forgetting to hand it to the maid. Thankfully, the lines he had so diligently practiced earlier came to him. "Miss Elizabeth, I trust you are in good health?"

"I have a headache," she responded weakly.

Her eyes did look a bit feverish. Darcy nodded, not knowing how to proceed. Should he send for the apothecary? "I—I had hoped to find you recovered." He bit his stammering lips together and mustered his composure. "I am sorry to hear otherwise." He managed a small smile at her, which she was too ill to return.

Wishing to ease her discomfort, he added, "My aunt's housekeeper keeps a well-stocked still room. I shall ask her to send a tonic for you."

"Thank you, Mr. Darcy." Elizabeth's tone was cool, civil. Her pain must be great indeed.

It occurred to him that now might not be the best time to make an offer. However, there was also the very real possibility that his proposal would be just the thing to ease Elizabeth's concerns and cure her ills. Who would not wish to distance themself from such a scandalous family as the Bennets? Live a life of luxury free of concerns?

The silence in the room grew awkward. Darcy shuffled his hat in his hands. Behind him, he heard the maid open the outer door, and he elected to seize the moment of privacy.

Clutching his hat, he closed the distance to stand directly in front of Elizabeth. With trembling hands and shaking voice, he began, "In vain I have struggled. It will not do."

A stifled scream interrupted him, and the sound of nails scrambling over carpetless floors erased the rehearsed words from his memory.

He turned to see a white dog charging him. Panic turned to agitation at the oafish puppy—tongue lolling, ears too big for its body, disproportionate paws clawing at the wood floors. He shouted for the undisciplined pup to heel, but the animal paid him no heed. The creature jumped on Darcy, pawing at his pressed cream breeches with muddy feet… and thoroughly ruining his proposal.

CHAPTER 2

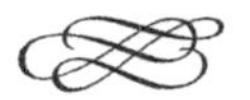

Elizabeth Bennet dropped her letters onto the table, grateful for the intrusion. (The dog's —*not* Mr. Darcy's.)

"Heel! Sit!" He pointed at the floor at his feet, his voice stern.

In a flagrant (and adorably sweet) display of disobedience, the puppy licked and nibbled at his fingers, insistently raking the front of his impeccably brushed and pressed breeches with her muddy paws.

It served him right. His unwelcome presence certainly had not improved Elizabeth's headache. Until now. The expression of absolute horror and disgust on Mr. Darcy's face made her hold her breath lest a delighted and slightly vengeful giggle escape.

Calling the dog over with low whistles and clucks, Elizabeth patted her legs and clapped to get the puppy's attention. It was not until Elizabeth crouched down on the floor that the Dane noticed her. She trotted over to sniff Elizabeth's skirts and lean into her hands when she scratched behind the puppy's ears.

She was a spindly thing—all ears and feet, with a sleek, white coat and black splotches on her rump and over one ear. Elizabeth rubbed behind her ears, talking in a soothing tone. "I am delighted to make your acquaintance, little miss. However did you find your way here? Did you escape from the kennels? Your blue eyes would be the envy of many ladies of my acquaintance. Yes, you are a beautiful girl, no doubt a gem among puppies! The kennel keeper will want to know how you escaped, and I fear you will not like your punishment very much. What does he call you, I wonder?"

The puppy nudged the ruby necklace at Elizabeth's throat, entirely unconcerned about the consequences of her escape.

"You like my necklace, do you? It is a ruby, a similar shade to your lovely pink nose." She ruffled the dog's fur, teasing, "Now, there is a name! Rambunctious Ruby. Is that what I shall call you?"

As Elizabeth felt Ruby licking her wrist, she looked up to see Mr. Darcy standing in the farthest corner, watching her and the dog, as composed as a gentleman accustomed to perfection could be with mud-stained breeches.

What had he wished to tell her? Whatever it was, it would wait for another day. She could not imagine what was so important he would call in the evening when he should have been dining with his aunt.

Elizabeth certainly had nothing to say to him. Nothing kind. Not after what he had done to separate Mr. Bingley from Jane. Colonel Fitzwilliam had been a veritable fount of knowledge. "Strong objections to the lady," indeed!

The gentleman opened his mouth, but before he could utter a word, there was a loud knock at the door. The maid soon joined them with the kennel keeper. Mr. Mansell doffed his hat and ducked his head. "My deepest apologies."

Elizabeth did not know if it was the work of her active imagination, the poor lighting in the room, or a valid observation, but the man paled at the sight of Mr. Darcy. "I am very sorry, sir," he mumbled as he passed the stuffy, disapproving gentleman. Grabbing Ruby by the scruff of her neck, he pulled her away.

Elizabeth rose to her feet, brushing off her hands. "She meant no harm."

"She never does." Mr. Mansell's smile was sad. He looped a lead around her head and pulled her closer to the door.

Mr. Darcy glared at the man, his tone sharp. "Is this a common occurrence?"

"It is the first time she has escaped her pen." Mr. Mansell sighed and rubbed his free hand over his face. "I had best return her to the kennel. My apologies, Mr. Darcy, Miss Bennet."

Ruby tugged against the lead, raising up on her back feet and making a cute squeaky noise as if she wished to give her regards to Mr. Darcy, who did not look impressed to be the recipient of the dog's attentions.

Mr. Darcy stepped away, hands crossed over his chest. "A Great Dane," he mumbled under his breath, as though the breed were a curse.

Ruby did not seem to understand she was in trouble. She trotted away, her tail whipping back and forth happily, a stark contrast to her keeper's sad expression.

Mr. Darcy watched them go, his gaze glued to the puppy, until the maid handed him a clean cloth with which to brush off mud from the breeches his valet would have to attend to later. With a bow, he took his leave from the parlor to the entrance hall. God forbid the great man would have to cross the lawn in muddy breeches. It did her humor good to observe the great Mr. Darcy seeing to such a humble task.

Feeling much better than she had minutes before, Elizabeth turned to the window and the pile of Jane's letters resting on the table in front of it. Poor Jane! If only Mr. Darcy had not influenced Mr. Bingley to leave Netherfield Park. What right had he to interfere? She pressed her fingers against her temples, the pounding beginning anew.

The source of her malaise bowed to take his leave. Good riddance.

"Mansell!" The voice coming from the other side of

the window drew her attention away from the disagreeable gentleman.

From the soft glow of the moon, Elizabeth saw Mr. Mansell on the path leading out to Hunsford's gate. His shoulders rose to his ears. His head tipped toward the puppy prancing at his feet, and his entire posture slumped in defeat.

The same voice she had heard a moment before sounded. "I told you to get rid of her." It was the gamekeeper, Mr. Fowler.

Surely Mr. Fowler did not mean what Elizabeth suspected. She moved closer to the door, where Mr. Darcy still stood in the shadows of the entrance. Fortunately, his attention was not on her but on the two other men.

Mr. Mansell bowed his head. "I have only to find a way to teach her, and she will be an exemplary specimen. Look at her lines, her size. She is a beauty."

"She is untrainable."

"In all fairness, sir, her training has only started."

"She does not look at you when you speak. The other puppies have learned to acknowledge your voice, but she does as she pleases. I have never seen a more rebellious dog." Mr. Fowler pulled a bag off his shoulder and handed it to Mr. Mansell. "She will discredit Her Ladyship's kennel. The problem must be dealt with whether you like it or not."

"No!" Elizabeth gasped. How could he be so cruel?

The two men turned to face her, and she stepped

around Mr. Darcy to give Mr. Fowler a piece of her mind.

Mr. Darcy beat her to it. "Surely Mr. Mansell should be given sufficient time to train the dog first." His haughty tone suited the occasion perfectly and her vexation at his interruption turned to triumph when Mr. Fowler stiffened and cleared his throat.

"Her Ladyship is particular about defective animals. They reflect poorly on her estate."

Mr. Darcy turned to Mr. Mansell, ignoring the gamekeeper. "How old is she?"

"Just over ten weeks, sir."

"When did her instruction begin?"

"Two weeks ago."

Mr. Fowler interrupted. "Something is wrong with the dog. No amount of training will beat that out of her."

"I should hope that beating is not necessary." Mr Darcy stood taller, his tone as imposing as his posture. Too bad he was not as considerate to people. "Young puppies require consistent direction over a long period of time. You cannot rightly determine that this one is without hope when her training has only just begun."

"Forgive me, Mr. Darcy, but your aunt has entrusted me with keeping the game at Rosings, and the kennels are under my authority. If she has any cause for complaint, she will take the matter up with me."

Mr. Darcy held up his hand. "You fulfill your role

admirably, Mr. Fowler. The streams teem with fish. There is ample game at my aunt's table, and during my rides over the property, I have yet to see a poacher's snare."

The gamekeeper softened his stance and, with a healthier measure of affability than he had demonstrated when he first arrived, he bowed his departure along with Mr. Mansell.

Mr. Darcy, too, bowed, his eyes pinched and his mouth bunched. With an exhale that communicated resignation, he said, "I shall speak with my aunt's housekeeper so she can send you some of her tonic. I wish you a prompt recovery."

"Thank you, Mr. Darcy. That is… kind of you." The praise stuck in her throat, but she forced it out. As she watched him catch up to the other men and continue down the path away from Hunsford, Elizabeth marveled at how quickly Mr. Darcy had gone from severe displeasure at the misbehaving Dane to rising in her defense.

Returning to the parlor, she collected her letters and went upstairs to her room. Elizabeth's headache subsided before Mr. Darcy sent the housekeeper's tonic, but her heart still ached for Jane.

CHAPTER 3

Having secured Mr. Fowler's word to give the errant pup more time, Darcy now felt at liberty to stomp back to Rosings to lick his wounded pride.

He had panicked. At a puppy.

Now that he knew that Ruby posed no danger to him, his fear had yielded to embarrassment and, finally, to frustration. It was harder for him to remain angry at the excitable miscreant now that Elizabeth had given her a name, but Darcy gave it his best effort.

He found the housekeeper in the kitchen. Elizabeth's tonic secured, he tread softly upstairs to avoid his aunt's notice, ruing the day gawky Ruby had taken it upon herself to ruin his proposal… and his breeches.

Chalmers poked the fire in the bedchamber to life. "I had the cook set aside a tray. Shall I send for it?" He faced Darcy and, with the improved light, saw the ruination of the fabric he had painstakingly brushed and pressed minutes before. His eyes pinched slightly and the corners of his lips spasmed, but Chalmers was too discreet to voice his thoughts.

An explanation was in order. He owed Chalmers that. "I had an incident with a boisterous escapee from the kennels."

"I shall see to them immediately." He pulled another more comfortable pair of breeches from the top of the dressing screen. Darcy donned them, glad to be rid of all signs of Ruby's intrusion.

He sat beside the fire and tended to his dinner tray, feeling his muscles uncoil and relax as he assessed the damage. He had decided to propose to Elizabeth and would not allow a rambunctious dog to spoil his plan.

Elizabeth had taken an immediate liking to Ruby and, upon reflection, Darcy determined that he had not uttered any unfavorable epithets aloud. In fact, his manners toward the dog, especially under the circumstances, could only recommend him to the lady. It would be easier for him to strike up a conversation with her at their next meeting. Perhaps she would tease him about the interloper, and he could say something charming about the playful pup. Really, that was all Ruby was. She was too young to be of any harm. This knowledge and the fact that Darcy had no reason to ever see Ruby again made him more forgiving.

Feeling more hopeful for the morrow—his last full day and night at Rosings before returning to London—

Darcy sipped tea and read from a book not likely to keep him up past his usual time to retire. One could only dwell on irrigation methods for so long before the eyelids became heavy.

Hours later, he was jarred awake by a kick at the door. He groggily arose and opened it to find Richard clutching a decanter in one hand and two glasses in the other.

"Uncle Lewis kept a fine cellar in his day." His cousin entered without invitation and sank into the chair opposite Darcy. Pouring brandy into the glasses, he handed one over. "Aunt Catherine was most displeased with your absence. You shall hear of nothing else on the morrow."

Darcy regretted provoking her over what amounted to nothing. However, he had never been one to be swayed by the opinion of his imperious aunt, and he was not about to begin now. "It shall be a welcome reprieve from her usual complaint."

"You and Anne?"

"What else?" Darcy groaned. One innocent comment from his mother about how well he and Anne played together as infants, and his aunt had taken it upon herself to assume an attachment. Her expectation had grown with each passing year until she was convinced that such an arrangement had been made at their birth. Unfortunately, Aunt did not take kindly to change, or Darcy would have succeeded in disabusing her of such a disagreeable engagement years ago.

Richard leaned forward, eyes gleaming with mischief. "Have you seen how Anne looks at her physician? It is no wonder she is so often ill."

Darcy had not, although he was not surprised his cousin had. There were few things that slipped past Richard's notice. "I wish her well with whomever she chooses."

"So long as she does not choose you!" Richard cackled. Darcy raised his drink, and they drank to the frustration of their aunt's plans. Richard topped off their glasses. "Has Miss Bennet's headache improved?"

Darcy nearly spilled his brandy in his haste to set it down on the table.

Richard chuckled. "You forget how often we have called at the parsonage since her arrival. You fancy her."

"Am I so obvious?"

"Hardly! An onlooker would never suspect. In fact, given your reticence, I doubt that the lady herself suspects your regard."

"Surely not!" Darcy shifted his weight, Richard's claim as uncomfortable as his chair.

Richard snorted. "The day I see you flirt with a young lady is the day you shall see me flouncing down the lane with an ostrich feather stuffed in my hat."

Darcy scowled, contemplating all the conversations he had enjoyed with Elizabeth at Netherfield Park, their snappy exchanges, the times their paths had crossed during her walks over the park, the set they had danced at Bingley's ball. Too many times, their eyes met over the table in his aunt's parlor. "Miss Elizabeth can be in no doubt of my regard."

"Really? How is that? Because you condescend to speak to her at all?"

Darcy did not dignify Richard's sarcasm with a reply.

"Because you sit stiffly on the parsonage settee and drink Mrs. Collins' tea while you listen to us converse for the appropriate fifteen minutes allotted to general acquaintances? It is a wonder Miss Elizabeth does not swoon at your mere presence!"

Darcy had allowed Richard quite enough fun at his expense. Flipping the tables, he commented, "At least my conversation does not leave her with a pounding headache."

Richard's smile melted. "Yes, I had opportunity between Aunt Catherine's counsel and Mr. Collins' supercilious praise to consider if perhaps it was something I said which might have provoked her discomfort. Miss Bennet is one to jest, and I understood her conversation as such, but I might have misread her reaction."

Elizabeth was always ready with a smile and a witty retort. It was one of the qualities Darcy most admired about her. He could not count on his fingers all the times she had teased him. She had even poked fun at him for not dancing at the assembly in her comments to Richard. "You have sketched her character well in so short a time."

"Still, as my father always counsels us, it is not for a man to understand the heart of a woman. It would be the height of pride for me to presume insight when I have no basis for such a claim."

How Uncle could utter that nonsense after over thirty years of marriage astounded Darcy. Did he not know his own wife? Darcy had determined that he would do better. Nestling against the back of his chair, he reached for his brandy. "What did you discuss? Perhaps I might help you discern whether you have cause for concern."

"We only spoke of Bingley."

Darcy sat forward. "Bingley? What could you possibly have to say about him?"

"Do not tell me you were not congratulating yourself on having lately saved—and I quote—'a friend from the inconveniences of a most imprudent marriage.' Who other than Bingley would get himself into a scrape of that sort? And after you had spent the whole of last summer with him at Netherfield."

Darcy grimaced. He had never intended for Elizabeth to learn of his interference, but a union to a family such as the Bennets would be the ruin of gullible, easily swayed Bingley. His friend did not have the strength of character to withstand the overbearing family, and for what? A tepid love from an indifferent wife? Bingley had asked for his opinion, and Darcy had replied honestly. He refused to regret his interference when it had been sought. "What else did you say?" He braced himself.

"Miss Bennet asked for your reasons for this interference. I merely told her my understanding." Richard shrugged.

"Which was?"

"That there were some very strong objections against the lady."

Darcy pressed his fingers against his temples, which had begun to throb. "And you did not notice any change in Miss Elizabeth's manners at this?"

Another shrug. "She enjoys a good jest. When she asked what arts you used to separate them, I initially assumed she was teasing. She prompted me to continue."

"I imagine she did." Darcy scoffed, his confidence in her regard wavering. Elizabeth was clever to extract all the information she wished, smiling prettily while his oafish cousin revealed every damning morsel. "How did you reply?"

"I said that you did not talk to me of your own arts, and that she now knew everything I did. Surely you can take no offense at that." Richard frowned and sipped from his glass. "However, I have to wonder... She did say that your conduct did not suit her feelings. She asked why you were to be the judge, what right you had to decide on the propriety of Bingley's inclination, and why, upon your judgment alone, you determined and directed in what manner Bingley was to be happy."

Darcy clenched his jaw. He thought his head might explode. "And you did not sense her pique?"

"I might have sooner had she not expressed her consideration, saying it was not to be supposed that there was much affection in the case. I commiserated, adding—in jest, mind you—that it lessened the honor of your triumph very sadly."

Ignorant dunderhead! Of all the things he could have said to Elizabeth, the fool had stumbled upon the one subject certain to foment her ire.

Richard downed the last of his brandy. "I suppose you had to be there. I praised you most effectively, holding you up as a model of exemplary friendship."

Darcy stopped his cousin before he could congratulate himself further. "The young lady I separated from Bingley was her sister."

Richard coughed, spraying Darcy as he gagged and stuttered. "H-her sis-ter?"

With the aim of increasing his cousin's guilt, Darcy added, "I had every intention of making an offer of marriage to Miss Elizabeth this evening."

Richard poured another glass, spilling over the edge in his haste, and downed it in one gulp. Darcy held his peace while Richard cleared his throat, no doubt preparing to utter an apology. Instead, he slammed his glass on the table and exclaimed, "Darcy! How could you?"

Darcy sucked in his breath, too stunned to reply.

"How is one Bennet unsuitable for Bingley when you would attach yourself to a family you deem objectionable? I have never known you to be such a hypocrite."

Darcy jerked back as though he had been struck. "Miss Bennet demonstrated no particular regard for him."

"An observation anyone might make about your regard for Miss Elizabeth!"

"Would you have Bingley marry without love?" He had to make Richard understand that he had acted as a good friend should, with Bingley's best interests at heart.

"And you determined Miss Bennet's motives by what means?"

Darcy folded his arms over his chest, certain that he was on firmer ground. He prided himself on being an excellent judge of character. "Through months of observation."

Richard rolled his eyes. "Since when were you granted the ability to read a lady's heart? Is not Bingley's happiness his own choice? Who made you the judge?"

"Bingley sought me out himself and asked for my opinion."

"Which you gladly gave, knowing how easily persuaded he is by you. He trusts you!" Richard shook his head. "I never thought I would see the day you abused that trust."

Darcy reeled as Richard continued mercilessly, "Tell me, has your counsel brought Bingley happiness, or has he been miserable since leaving Hertfordshire?"

Sucking in a deep breath, Darcy suddenly felt sick. He had spoken the truth and answered honestly when Bingley had asked his opinion. This should not be happening.

"And the young lady. Darcy, what if you were wrong about Miss Bennet? From the little I know of her family, you have dealt them a harsh blow, depriving Miss Bennet of a beneficial match to a gentleman who would graciously care for her and her family." Richard scrubbed his hand over his face. "It was fortuitous you did not propose to Miss Elizabeth tonight, I can promise you that. She would certainly have refused you."

Over a matter that could so easily be resolved? He would simply tell her the truth–that he had spoken at Bingley's request. He had told the truth as he knew it. He had been honest, for heaven's sake!

To Darcy's chagrin, Richard had more to say on the subject. "I am appalled by your lack of consideration toward a worthy lady you claim to love. Did you not think how Aunt Catherine would react if she found out you made an offer to someone other than Anne while residing as her guest? How she would punish the Collinses for inviting Miss Elizabeth here? Our aunt is capable of introducing more misery than they have ever known in their lives, and for what? So you can congratulate yourself on your condescension? Create more mayhem in Miss Elizabeth's family, as though you have not caused enough? It is unconscionable!"

Richard's face twisted in disgust—a look he had never before directed at Darcy, who felt his cousin's censure like a kick in the ribs.

Darcy continued to sit by the fire in numb silence, only stirring long after Richard left the room and when Chalmers returned to assist him out of his coat and into his nightclothes. He struggled to understand his error, but he could not deny the truth of Richard's accusations.

All that mattered right now was what Elizabeth thought. If she considered him the destroyer of her sister's happiness, then there was only one thing to do. Somehow he must improve her opinion of him.

Angry at himself, angry at Richard, and angry at the circumstances which had upset Elizabeth, Darcy stayed awake several hours longer committing his thoughts to paper.

He thanked Heavens for Ruby, or he would never have had the opportunity to explain himself to the woman he loved.

CHAPTER 4

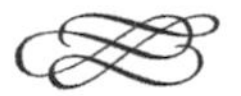

Not since Arthur Wellesley's well-deserved promotion to general the year before had Colonel Richard Fitzwilliam been so frustrated with his lot. It had been Richard's choice not to join his comrade on the continent, but every day his unfulfilled desire to do something of import— to make a name for himself—tormented him like an itch he could not reach.

What had Richard gained for this agony? A happy mother and a grateful father. No challenge to meet. No adversary to conquer. No respected ally to assist to glory. Just his small band of men, each soldier Richard ensured was as competent as himself. And his family… including his pain-in-the-backside cousin Darcy.

Richard squeezed his fingers into tight fists, feeling his skin stretch over his knuckles and his nails bite into his fleshy palms. It had been many years since he had felt this angry. Angry with his circumstances. Angry with himself. Angry with Darcy for reflecting a glimpse of the arrogance so common in their circles. How could he be such a conscientious landlord, loyal friend, and responsible gentleman and tout such pompous nonsense?

He marched into his bedchamber and closed the door, taking a deep breath. He must be fair. Known for his generosity and loyalty, Darcy was surrounded by untrustworthy peers intent on gaining his friendship.

That Darcy saw beyond the usual allurements of wealth, prestige, and position to recognize the qualities which would make a lady a good wife did him credit—as much as it recommended Miss Elizabeth. She must be truly extraordinary. Richard's impression was already favorable. Had she possessed even a smallish fortune, he would not have hesitated to pursue her himself. Though he cursed his cousin's high-handed interference and arrogant foolishness, he wished to see Darcy happy and settled with a woman he would not come to regret. If he did not bungle his chances first.

Richard had never seen Darcy in love before this. It would seem that his cousin's effectiveness in managing his estates, properties, and army of servants had done nothing to facilitate the management of his own heart. Contemplating Darcy's behavior toward Miss Elizabeth over more than a fortnight of their mutual proximity in Kent, Richard concluded that the lady had no perception of his cousin's regard. Even with the advantage of knowing Darcy better than anyone, *he* had been ignorant of his designs.

He chuckled to himself. That was one notable mark in Miss Elizabeth's favor: She paid no heed to Darcy.

Another point in her favor: She laughed often—at herself as much as others' follies. She laughed at Darcy too. And he bore it well. Better than when Richard made him the butt of a joke. Richard chuckled. Darcy probably thought she was flirting with him, the dunderhead.

Pulling the curtains aside, Richard rubbed his jaw and peered through the glass across the lawns toward Hunsford Cottage.

Miss Elizabeth had spoken plainly about the poor impression Darcy had made on her, her family, and the entire village of Meryton. Amazingly, Darcy had taken no offense. Imagine what Miss Elizabeth could do to improve Darcy's character if she actually tried; if she understood her influence!

She was not a fortune hunter, or she would have batted her eyelashes and flattered Darcy's boorish conduct as freely as the other ladies of the *ton*. She smiled often, but she was not a flirt. Not unless her version of feminine arts involved calling out a man's behavior and putting him in his place with her quick wit—as Richard had observed her do so skillfully, revealing Darcy's refusal to dance at a public assembly short on partners even as her nimble fingers plucked at the keys of Aunt Catherine's pianoforte.

This was the woman Darcy would have!

Humor triumphed over dissatisfaction, and Richard roared with laughter. Oh, the irony! Darcy would fall in love with the only woman in Christendom who would not have him!

He nursed a glass of his uncle's finest and watched the embers in the fireplace die as he recalled every conversation and exchange he had enjoyed with Miss Elizabeth since his arrival to Rosings. It did not take him long to see that the benefit to Darcy in securing Miss Elizabeth's affection actually exceeded the advantages Darcy could offer her.

Richard also determined that, while she was a gentleman's daughter, her character portrayed none of the weak-mindedness or greedy ambition so common among their set. She was not intimidated by Aunt Catherine and often used humor to dispel the great lady's rude questions. The heat of society's opposition would only strengthen her (and they would oppose her with all the ferocity of a thousand rejected maidens and their scorned mothers).

But what of Darcy? His character was firm, but he was blind if he thought society would accept Miss Elizabeth merely because he chose her. His ignorance would hurt her, and Darcy would despise himself for it. He did not take his failures lightly. If Miss Elizabeth was to be tested, should not Darcy also be put to the test? He was doggedly persistent for a cause, loyal to his trustworthy friends, and constant in his regard... but would he be all those things for Miss Elizabeth?

Downing the last of the liquid in the glass, Richard came to a conclusion. If he was stuck in England when he would rather forge a glorious military career on the continent, then he would find a fight worth engaging in here. He could think of no battle more worthy than helping his favorite cousin, his closest friend, win the heart of a worthy woman.

From the look of things, Darcy needed all the help Richard could give him.

CHAPTER 5

After several wasted pages and wasted hours, Darcy decided that enough was enough, signed his name at the bottom of his letter, and crawled into bed. He was wealthy, not wasteful—of time or stationery.

The penned lines haunted him and stole his sleep. It was with relief that the first glimmer of dawn lightened his room and spread across the floor. Dressing and shaving himself, Darcy tucked the letter inside his pocket, eager to rid himself of it.

Richard, an inveterate early riser, was already in the breakfast parlor with a plate piled with savory cuts of meat, which he devoured with rolls generously garnished with rhubarb preserves. Darcy only poured coffee to drink. His aunt's table was always generously rationed, but his stomach was too perturbed for food.

Dabbing his mouth with one hand, Richard poured

cream into his coffee with the other. "I had thought to check on our furry little friend this morning."

Feeling charitable after the blunder from which the puppy had saved him, Darcy agreed to accompany him. He drew the line, however, at calling the half-baked beast a "friend." However, to be fair, the miniature monster had done him a good turn. Wrapping a couple of rashers of bacon into his handkerchief to offer as a reward—whether for himself once he successfully handed his letter to Miss Elizabeth or for the puppy as a mark of gratitude remained to be ascertained—Darcy waited impatiently for his cousin to finish his meal.

Like him, Elizabeth made good use of the early hours, often taking long walks over the park. If they hastened, they might see her. And if they were merely walking Ruby, Darcy had the perfect excuse to cross paths with her. She might even be pleased to see... the dog.

Not him. Not yet.

He *would* change her opinion of him, and much as he despised the delay, such a feat would take some time. He would give her the letter, then he would depart the following day for London as planned. A week of pondering over his words should suffice. Elizabeth possessed a quick mind. Any longer than a week would only delay their happiness. He merely had to give her the letter. With every step down the sloping lawn, it burned hotter in Darcy's pocket.

"For whom are you looking?" Richard looked

askance at Darcy, brow raised, lips in a poorly concealed smile. As if he knew the answer full well and only asked to poke fun.

Darcy ignored him. They were near the kennels.

"I doubt Miss Elizabeth would walk so close to the house, knowing you to be in residence." Richard grinned at his own joke.

"No thanks to you," Darcy growled.

Richard raised his hands. "Kill not the messenger. While I deeply regret my role in your current predicament, let us not forget who originated the cause of your lady's distress." He stared pointedly at Darcy.

Darcy glared at the numbskull. What kind of friend would he be if he did not speak the truth? If he allowed Bingley to form an unequal attachment? He had saved his friend from years of misery and regret. "You should wish I would be as forthright with you as I was with Bingley."

"Now, that is rich! Did you write *that* in your letter?" Richard laughed at his cousin's obvious astonishment. "Do not look so surprised, Darcy. You never choose to speak what you can pen to paper for reference, thus avoiding the need to repeat yourself or offer any further explanation."

Darcy frowned. "I think better on paper." Especially when Elizabeth was near. She had a way of muddling his thoughts when he was in her company.

Rolling his eyes, Richard gibed, "And did you write your explanation with the expectation of earning Miss

Elizabeth's gratitude? Perhaps an apology for her misunderstanding?"

"Of course not." Darcy knew Elizabeth well enough to be certain no apology would be forthcoming. A bit of gratitude, though, would be appropriate.

Mansell clanged a metal spoon against the side of a soup pot; happy barks greeted him as he entered the kennel. He dropped a large spoonful of what looked like a stew of fine-pollard, carrots, parsnips, and chunks of meat in the bowl at his feet by the first dog. The eager hunter lapped it up greedily as Mansell continued down the line.

Darcy swallowed his fear and followed Richard inside, doing his level best not to stare at the humongous beasts devouring their meal. They would make quick work of him. Perhaps the bacon in his pocket was not such a brilliant idea. He pressed against the opposite wall as closely as possible without looking ridiculous, keeping within arm's reach of Mansell and Richard. He had dogs at Pemberley. There was no logical reason for him to fear the oversized hounds feeding not three feet away from him. Clearing his throat, he asked, "Have the puppies been fed?"

"Fed them first. This is the second batch." Mansell spoke as he spooned out generous portions into the bowls. His kennel was as clean as could be expected, and he greeted each inhabitant by name. His charges received him with wagging tails, soft ears, relaxed eyes, and open, smiling mouths full of pointy teeth (at which Darcy tried very hard not to stare). Each animal waited to eat until given the command signal.

Darcy admired the kennel keeper's skill (all the better to keep his mind off the kennel residents). "You have their obedience and affection."

Richard jabbed Darcy in the arm with his elbow. "What is your secret to inspire such obedience, Mansell? I could use it on the new recruits."

Mansell chuckled softly. "The way to a man's heart is through his stomach… much the same as a dog."

"Mankind has gone to the dogs! My mother would never forgive me if I stole off with her cook." Richard patted his stomach and nodded at the puppies' pen. "Is the little fugitive my cousin met last night in? We should like to take her for a stroll around the park."

The trainer whistled, and all the puppies looked at him—except one, Darcy noticed. Ruby continued sniffing the ground until she noticed her brothers' and sisters' reactions.

Something in Darcy's chest tightened. He tried to blame the coffee—he knew better than to drink the brew on an empty stomach. But a suspicion took root in his mind. It nagged at him as Mansell described the extent of her leash training to Richard. Motioning at the splotched white Dane, he asked, "Is she—"

His question was interrupted by the arrival of Fowler. The dogs did not seem as happy to see him. Their displeasure changed the air in the kennel. Darcy would save his question for later. It would not do to bring it up in front of Fowler.

Taking the lead from Mansell and accepting the kind man's thankful expression with a nod, Darcy looped the leather over Ruby's head and tugged her out of the kennel while Richard clucked his tongue and whistled for her to follow. Glancing over his shoulder to see Fowler watching them, Darcy walked faster. He had to get Ruby away from that man.

"Slow down, Darcy! You will strangle the poor girl." Richard snapped the lead away from him.

Pointing toward the most expedient path away from the kennel, Darcy reached into his pocket and broke off a piece of bacon. "Let us continue down this lane." He tossed the bacon above the pup's head, and Ruby made a valiant effort to catch it in mid-air. She jumped, only to have the meat slap against her nose and land on the grass, where she was finally able to gobble up her treat.

"She is a lovable animal, is she not? Even if she is a Great Dane?" Richard ruffled her ears.

"The flaw of her breed aside, she is endearing." Darcy pulled the letter from his pocket. If they chanced upon Elizabeth, he would waste no time giving it to her.

"Let me guess. Is that the bitter justification you spent all night writing?"

Flicking the paper in his hand as though it would catch fire, anxious and hating his own uncertainty,

Darcy glowered at his cousin. Why he endured Richard's impertinence was a mystery. Yet he was Darcy's best friend.

Richard rose to his feet. "Heel," he commanded Ruby, who had been contentedly sniffing the ground for more bacon until she noticed the gleaming white envelope Darcy smacked nervously against his leg.

Quicker than Darcy could react, the dog lunged, grabbing the paper and tugging it out of his hand. He managed to retrieve it before she tore it to bits. He held the soggy envelope between the tips of his fingers as a blob of drool trailed a path down the side and plopped on the tip of his boot. Ruby jumped and pawed, straining against Richard's hold. "Down! Heel!" Darcy found himself saying, though he did not know why he bothered.

How many of his plans did this impertinent whelp mean to destroy? He could not give this slobber coated letter to Miss Elizabeth. Nor could he be so cruel to Chalmers as to stuff it back inside his pocket until it had sufficiently dried. Not when his valet would already be cross because of the smell of bacon.

"Oh no," Darcy groaned. The bacon had been in the same pocket as the letter. No wonder Ruby had grabbed at it.

She spun in a circle, her entire back end wiggling, her grin wide.

"This is not a game, you naughty minx." Darcy did not have the heart to scold her beyond a mild reproof when the fault had mostly been his. Her eyes were too fixed on the bacon-scented letter to heed his words. Drat it all. It was only a matter of time before Fowler noticed.

Richard guffawed. "She seems to think otherwise. See how she pays you no mind? A female with a superior intellect!"

Darcy tried to get her attention, praying he was wrong. Snapping his fingers, he called, "Ruby! Up here, Ruby. Look up here." He snapped by his face, but she did not look away from the mouth-watering letter in his other hand for longer than a blink.

Drat.

"Ruby? You have named her?"

Fixing his cousin with another stern scowl, Darcy explained, "The dog took a fancy to Miss Elizabeth's ruby necklace, and the lady commented on it. The name stuck in my mind. That is all."

"You mean you have not yet lost your heart to this young lady?" Richard knelt down, playfully squishing Ruby's cheeks. "Who could deny this adorable little face?"

"It will not stay little much longer. She is already bigger than Aunt Catherine's lap dog, and a year from now, she will weigh as much as you do."

"Not all Great Danes grow into fearsome, territorial beasts. In a good home—"

Darcy raised his hand. He had seen Elizabeth, and

he was done with this conversation. "I will have no Great Danes on Pemberley property, and that is final."

Leaving Richard with his new friend, Darcy tucked the soggy letter back in his pocket with a silent apology to Chalmers and hastened down the path to greet Elizabeth.

It was not until he had caught her attention and noticed her brow raised in marked disapproval that he remembered that he could no longer rely on his original plan. He could not hand her a drool-soaked letter and bid his leave with a dignified bow.

He would have to talk to her.

Drat that dog!

CHAPTER 6

Elizabeth took note of the location of the nearest tree and wondered how conspicuous it would look if she were to run the short distance to hide behind it. Much too obvious, she concluded with a sigh of resignation. There was no avoiding him. She would have to speak with Mr. Darcy.

From the moment he had described her as merely tolerable and refused to dance with her or anyone else at the assembly, her attitude toward the "gentleman" had leaned toward dislike—and the dislike subsequently strengthened based upon his history with Mr. Wickham, his high-handed interference with Mr. Bingley, and his arrogant disdain for anyone outside the pitifully small sphere of acquaintances he had condescended to grace with his approval.

"Good morning, Miss Elizabeth. I hope you are enjoying a pleasant walk."

She *had* been. She had previously noted his aversion to Lady Catherine's kennels and chose the path nearest the building today for that reason alone. Too polite to admit as much aloud, she nodded, her displeasure deepening when she saw Colonel Fitzwilliam and Ruby continuing down the path when she would have appreciated the addition of their company.

Mr. Darcy extended his arm to her, then (to his credit) seemed to think better of the gesture. Good. He had spared her the awkwardness of refusing.

"Miss Elizabeth, I have become aware of certain… events. Events which I… regret."

Elizabeth spun around to face him. Did he expect her to read his mind to understand his meaning? Desirous of keeping their interaction brief, she asked plainly, "Are you referring to Mr. Bingley and my sister Jane?"

He reached for his pocket, then dropped his hand, still empty. Elizabeth imagined him pulling out a cigar which he would light in front of her to better rub his triumph in her face, although the pained expression straining his eyes suggested otherwise. After some hesitation, he replied, "Yes."

Elizabeth steeled her nerves. While she recognized Mr. Darcy's pronounced discomfort, she felt herself under no obligation to abate his uneasiness. Why should she when he had not made the smallest effort toward her or anyone else in Meryton? "Tell me, Mr. Darcy, which troubles you the most? Is it the 'event'—

as you call it—that you regret, or the fact that I know about it?" Her tone sounded sharper to her own ears than she had intended, but she did not feel remorse.

His reluctance to answer was reply enough.

Taking a deep breath and mumbling a quick prayer for forbearance, Elizabeth continued walking before she yielded to the temptation to throttle him with her reticule (which, as usual, contained a book and would make an admirable weapon). To her chagrin, she heard his footsteps following. "Please, Miss Elizabeth, allow me to explain."

Now, *this* she would be interested to hear. She stopped short, letting him catch up to stand before her. How could he—the agent of her sister's unhappiness—possibly explain his presumption? She plopped her fists on her hips. "I am all ears, sir." It sounded like a taunt or a dare, which was precisely her intent.

He understood her manner, though he seemed puzzled by it. His brows furrowed in what would have been an endearing expression in any other man. He slipped off his hat and rubbed a hand through his dark, wavy tresses. Such a waste of perfect hair. Now he was wiping his palm against his breeches and clearing his throat.

Once again, he reached for his coat pocket but remained empty-handed. Elizabeth wondered what was contained in Mr. Darcy's pocket that he so often reached for. A flask of liquid boldness perhaps? A diverting notion, but Elizabeth dismissed it immediately. Mr. Darcy was not the sort of man to voluntarily lose control of his senses. Not without a compelling reason.

He took a deep breath. "Miss Bennet would not be the first handsome lady to whom Bingley has lost his heart in recent years."

"Did you separate him from them too?" Elizabeth snapped.

"On occasion."

"You take an exceeding interest in your friend's prospects, sir."

"Bingley is my friend. I could do no less."

"You believe his happiness is secure in your superior hands?"

"Those young ladies would not have made him happy. They were mercenary, out to deceive a trusting gentleman in possession of a fortune for their own security. I could not rightly stand by and watch him fall prey to a dishonest woman out to advance herself."

Elizabeth held her hands stiffly at her side, heat flooding her face. "Jane is not mercenary!"

Mr. Darcy held up his hand. "I merely intended to describe the ladies of the *ton* who have formed part of Bingley's past, not to include your sister among them."

"Then what *are* your objections?"

"Bingley's attachment appeared to me to be stronger than hers."

His tone was so matter-of-fact, Elizabeth's blood boiled. "Jane is modest!"

"And a good daughter, no doubt, who would do her duty by her family."

She choked back her retort. Jane *was* a good daughter, and Elizabeth could not dismiss the possibility that her dear sister would sacrifice her own happiness if she believed her family would benefit from it. Still, she could not allow Mr. Darcy to win this argument.

"What made you assume we wished for the connection?" She winced the moment the question crossed her tongue. Her mother had made the advantages of such a connection plain—emphatically plain.

"At the Netherfield Ball, Sir William suggested that Bingley's marked attentions to your sister had given rise to a general expectation of their marriage. He spoke of it as a certain event, a premature conclusion propagated by your mother, who frequently and vociferously praised the match." Gone was Mr. Darcy's awkward silence. He loomed over her, confident and vexed.

Elizabeth's cheeks burned with shame. Although she dearly wished to, she could not deny it.

"From that moment," he continued, "I observed my friend's behavior attentively, and I perceived that his partiality for Miss Bennet was beyond what I had ever witnessed in him."

She gasped. Mr. Bingley *did* love Jane. "If his intentions were honorable, why did you take it upon yourself to separate them? How could you possibly determine Jane's motive when she rarely expresses her feelings to me, her own sister?" Now that she had a more compelling argument, Elizabeth stretched herself to her full height and lifted her chin.

"Her look and manners were open, cheerful, and engaging as ever but without any symptom of peculiar regard—"

"Did you expect her to display some sort of love sickness? If symptoms are what you seek, might I remind you of the illness which kept her at Netherfield Park for nearly a week? Would a stuffy nose suffice? Or must a lady suffer a high fever and delirium too?" *Insufferable, unreasonable man!*

He crossed his arms over his chest. "I remained convinced after the evening's scrutiny that, though she received his attentions with pleasure, she did not invite them by any participation of the sentiment." His tone was deep and dangerous—the perfect combination to stir Elizabeth's ire fully.

Taking a step closer to him, she assumed her best glare and opened her mouth to let fly all the insults propriety had formerly prevented her from uttering. However, he spoke again before she pronounced so much as a syllable, this time with a more conciliatory tone and posture. "If you have not been mistaken, then *I* must have been in error. Your superior knowledge of your sister must make the latter probable."

Was that an apology? If so, it was a stuffy, pathetic attempt. With a huff, Elizabeth folded her hands over her chest and resumed walking. She had come too close to forgetting her manners, and she refused to stoop to Mr. Darcy's level by lashing out with insults.

Again, he chased after her. He was like a bur caught on her skirt that she could only expel with a great deal of pinching and prying.

"If that is the circumstance, then your resentment is not unreasonable."

Oh, how she wished she could pinch him! "Thank you, Mr. Darcy, for allowing me a degree of acrimony. You are too generous."

His forehead gathered into a deep V. "The serenity of your sister's countenance and the amiability of her temper might have convinced the most acute observer that her heart was not likely to be easily touched."

She rounded to face him. "A conviction you reached after one night of observation?" The pompous boor nodded. "You did not wish for my sister to snatch your friend away from Miss Darcy. Miss Bingley congratulates herself on the anticipated match just as you say my mother has done."

Mr. Darcy went pale. "Bingley and *my sister?* Miss Bingley said *that?*"

Recognizing his panic, Elizabeth prodded, "Unwilling for your sister to wed a family with connections to trade, Mr. Darcy?"

Eyes wide, mouth agape, he gawked at her. "It is simply not true. Georgiana would never—not after—" He clamped his mouth shut and swallowed in the manner of one about to fall ill.

Not wishing to witness such a revolting display, Elizabeth stepped away from the gentleman, turning the subject away from his sister and back to hers. "You conveniently saw what you wanted to see. And you used it to separate a pair who had every prospect of making each other happy."

Mr. Darcy seemed to grow taller. "That I was desirous of believing her indifferent is certain—"

"Ha! You admit it!"

"I believed it on impartial conviction, as truly as I wished it in reason."

Elizabeth bristled. "Reason? Do you consider Jane beneath him?"

"For a gentleman's daughter, she wants for connections. But this is not so great an evil to Bingley as it would be for a landed gentleman."

"A gentleman such as yourself?" Elizabeth seethed. "Do not fear, Mr. Darcy, you are quite safe from the females in my family. We would never presume more than the slightest acquaintance with one so grand as you, knowing how repugnant you find us."

The distance between them closed until they stood toe-to-toe. He towered over her, but she held his disdainful look with a glare of her own.

When he spoke, his voice was low and articulate. "The situation of your mother's family, though objectionable, is nothing in comparison of the total want of propriety so frequently, almost uniformly betrayed by herself, by your three younger sisters, and occasionally even by your father."

Elizabeth sucked in a breath. "Thank you for making your true feelings known so plainly. I will not spoil your day with my presence any longer." She turned away. She could not remain in his company a moment longer.

She felt his fingers brush against her elbow. Wrenching her arm out of reach, she glanced over her shoulder and saw him standing with his hands clasped in front of him, his head bowed. "Pardon me, Miss Elizabeth. It pains me to offend you."

This flicker of humility stopped her. "And yet you are so good at giving offense."

"It is not done—has never been done —intentionally."

Elizabeth did not know how to reply to that, nor could she summon her feet to obey her desire to walk away.

"Of my poor estimation, I must exclude you and your sister… if it is of any consolation."

It was. And Elizabeth hated that she cared enough about Mr. Darcy's opinion for his words to be of comfort. She felt as wretched as Jane had appeared since Mr. Bingley's departure.

Eyes burning, her throat thick, she said, "Jane went to London. She hoped to see him. Do you call that indifferent? She even called on Miss Bingley, hoping to at least retain that lady's friendship."

Mr. Darcy's head snapped up, his eyes intense. "She called?"

"Do not trouble yourself. Miss Bingley protected her brother from an unhappy circumstance as well as you would have done." Elizabeth knew she was pushing him, but her hurt for sweet, suffering Jane was too deep to allow the matter to drop until she was satisfied she had argued Jane's case sufficiently.

Apparently hanging onto his patience by a thread, Mr. Darcy said, "Miss Bingley was no more in favor of the match than I was. Once we joined Bingley in London, I readily engaged in the office of pointing out to my friend the certain evils of such a choice. I described and pressed them upon him earnestly."

I bet you did, Elizabeth thought ungraciously.

"However my remonstrance might have altered his determination, I do not believe it would ultimately have prevented him from returning to Hertfordshire had it not been seconded by the assurance—which I did not hesitate to give—of your sister's indifference. Bingley had believed her to return his affection with sincere, if not equal regard. He has a great natural modesty and a stronger dependence on my judgment than on his own. It was not difficult to convince him that he had deceived himself."

Elizabeth trembled with rage and the overwhelming desire to throttle Mr. Darcy. "You are wrong about Jane."

"So you have given me to understand, and now I

can no longer reflect on my conduct with satisfaction." Darcy looked down at the ground, appearing humble and embarrassed.

Her eyes widened, and she stared at him with something other than antipathy for the first time. Had he just apologized?

She would have expected to feel more satisfaction at such an extraordinary event. To bring the imperious man low enough to admit to an error, no matter how slight his admission, should have filled her to the brim with gratification. But all she felt was sadness. How could she be otherwise when Jane pined away in London over a man incapable of making up his own mind? Was Mr. Bingley even worthy of Jane? "The damage is done."

"If I have wounded your sister's feelings, it was unknowingly done. Though the motives which governed me may very naturally appear insufficient to you, I have not yet learned to condemn them."

Elizabeth could easily have taken offense at his admission, but his honesty (as unflattering as it was) surprised her, as did his insight into her thoughts. She *did* believe his motive was insufficient and presumptuous and haughty. While she would prefer to have remained angry with him, instead she felt terribly weary, wanting nothing more than to return to the parsonage.

Before she could excuse herself, and beg for him

not to follow, he spoke. "Of one artful disguise I can no longer excuse myself."

She could summon no question or retort.

"I knew Miss Bennet was in town, and I concealed it from Bingley. He is unaware of her proximity; of that I am certain." He raised a finger—whether to emphasize a point or to prevent her from interrupting, Elizabeth did not know. "I did not know she had called on Miss Bingley at his residence."

"Would it have signified?" Even her voice sounded weary.

"I would have been forced to amend my opinion about her indifference."

"Would you have gone to the same effort to convince Mr. Bingley of your error as you did in extracting him from Netherfield Park? Can such a thing be undone?"

Something in Mr. Darcy's eye and the determined set of his jaw told her he would have tried. While she heartily approved of his certitude—at least, when it was accurately directed—she was not yet ready to think kindly of the gentleman, so she quashed the thought.

CHAPTER 7

Elizabeth's indication of favor—a flash as quick as a bolt of lightning—nearly undid Darcy. He quivered inside with the force of her regard. Such was his reward for exposing his error, and Darcy grasped on to it with all the gratitude he possessed.

But it was not enough. Not when his feelings were so fully engaged. His heart had settled on Elizabeth to be his wife, but now his worst fear was confirmed. She did not love him. Worse, she could hardly tolerate him. During their brief exchange, he had seen expressed on her lovely visage a medley of emotions—anger, frustration, sadness… everything but what he most wished to see. Until that brief blink, that small flicker of approbation.

How deep was her disfavor to be unwilling to think him capable of kindness? He had thought her family repugnant, but to hear her use his own thoughts as ammunition, for him to bear her chastisement as she turned his arguments against him… it left Darcy reeling.

Could the damage be undone? she had asked. He prayed it could be. Battered and unsteady, he finally answered her question. "I do not know, but I must try."

Another flicker, a softening in her eyes. A whispered, "I believe you will."

His heart soared. How low he had been brought that such a trifling expression of her confidence would influence him at all. And yet, he must have more. He would earn her esteem if he had to crawl on his knees to Bingley's residence.

"Come back, you little minx!" Richard shouted.

Darcy saw the colonel waving his arms in the air, bounding after the agile dog, who dragged her lead behind her. Straight to him and Elizabeth.

Another interruption, although Darcy had to admit that this one was not so unwelcome as the former had initially been. When Elizabeth bent over and clapped her hands with a large smile directed at the escaped puppy, Darcy was glad Ruby had chosen that moment to intrude.

He saw the danger when, tongue lolling and intent on her new friend, Ruby was about to bowl into Elizabeth's skirts. Reaching for the female least likely to bite him, Darcy grasped Elizabeth's shoulders. In the next second, she fell back against his chest.

Enveloped in orange blossom and cinnamon, the

temptation to hold her close and inhale her intoxicating scent nearly triumphed over his good sense. His assistance was unwelcome. Quickly, before he could give in, he unhanded her.

He could not so easily shake the exhilarating effect of having the woman he adored in his arms for a brief moment. He held his breath, memorizing the smell of her hair. The soft velvet of her spencer lingered on his fingertips. Even the rosettes arranged in her bonnet continued to tickle his chin.

Running away from Darcy to a nearby tree, Elizabeth grabbed a stick, which she waved in front of the dog. The two engaged in a delightful game of tug-of-war. Richard joined in the fun, trying to tempt Ruby with a stick of his own. Darcy stood awkwardly off to the side. He could not join in their fun when his thoughts were so grave.

His resolve strengthened with every one of Elizabeth's smiles, each smile widening in its sincerity as all evidence of the melancholy and disappointed hopes on behalf of her sister—all of which he had caused—vanished. If Darcy's tendency was to hold on to resentment, Elizabeth was his opposite. Would she forgive him?

He would have Chalmers ready for an earlier departure than he had planned—this afternoon, if it was possible. Aunt Catherine would be sorely vexed, but there was no time to waste.

Richard tossed his stick into a hedge. "She has a strong grip for one so young."

Elizabeth yielded her stick to the triumphant Dane, who pranced at her side and slobbered on her trophy. Wiping her hands together, Elizabeth bobbed a curtsy. "It has been a pleasure, but I should return to the parsonage."

Stepping forward, Richard extended his arm. "Pray allow us to escort you, Miss Elizabeth. I had hoped to call on Mr. and Mrs. Collins before our departure on the morrow." He nodded at Ruby. "We can leave this young lady at the kennels along the way."

Elizabeth met Darcy's gaze, and he tried not to look too greedy for her company—not unlike Ruby, who looked up at the lady with complete devotion. Turning to the colonel, Elizabeth rested her hand against his arm. "Thank you, Colonel. How kind of you."

Still feeling the weight of Elizabeth's reprimands, Darcy bent down to catch the puppy's lead before she ran away again. He fell in behind Richard and Elizabeth and tried not to be jealous. She did not have the dowry Richard required, but her charm could easily convince a man that the lady herself was plenty of recompense. Darcy had been willing to overlook her family's indiscretions and circumstances.

Perhaps he ought not to have pointed them out so plainly. Certainly they were undeniable facts, but she had winced as he spoke them. His words had hurt her. Darcy had always taken pride in his honesty, but until today he had not considered how unkind his honesty had been. His candor had caused needless suffering to Bingley and Miss Bennet. Darcy's conviction had been strong, but he had been wrong. He had been ignorant of Miss Bennet's true feelings.

Was that where the fault lie? In his ignorance? He had thought he possessed all the facts. Until Elizabeth had pointed out the egregiousness of his error. He had no reason to doubt her. While he considered himself an excellent judge of character, he would not presume to know more about Miss Bennet's heart than her own sister, with whom she was undeniably close.

He pondered the implications during the walk back to the kennels. Richard and Elizabeth waited outside the large doors. Darcy strode past them in search of Mansell, straight into the kennel full of gigantic dogs with booming barks. He would assume nothing. From here on, he would ask for the facts.

Seeing him enter, Mansell joined him near the doors (which suited Darcy well, as it was easier to be brave when his exit was close). "I hope she did not give you too much trouble."

Too intent on his purpose for pleasantries, Darcy blurted, "You said Ruby will require more training and attention than the others in her litter. In what respect is she different?"

Mansell removed his hat, twisting and tugging it between his hands as he looked to collect his thoughts. "She is a fine canine in every aspect save one. If I can figure out how best to train her, if I could give her the time she requires, I am convinced she will obey as well as any other dog."

"Speak plainly, Mansell. Is the dog deaf?"

Darcy heard Elizabeth gasp behind him. Richard sighed. "Of course. How did I miss it?"

Bunching his cheeks, Mansell nodded. "Yes, that is the long and short of it."

"Have you trained a deaf dog before?" Darcy asked.

"No."

Neither had Darcy. He had nothing helpful to offer Mansell.

Elizabeth appeared at his side. "But there must be a way. She is perfectly lovely."

Mansell's smile expressed his sadness. "I agree, miss. However, most would see her difference as a burden. She will require a great deal more work than most dogs. She needs someone who is patient, persistent, who will not be swayed by public opinion, who is firm and willing to dedicate the requisite time and attention to properly train her. Someone with an ample and kind heart."

Darcy's pulse raced. A kind heart. He looked at Elizabeth, who was looking at Richard.

"I have no room in my apartments, nor time when I am on duty." A sensible reply, to be sure, but it rankled Darcy's sensibility that Elizabeth had thought of his cousin before considering himself. Did she believe him so cold and unfeeling?

Mansell continued, "Because she cannot hear, she is easily startled, and startled dogs are more inclined to bite."

This Darcy knew well. The reminder made him hesitate to do what he knew he must.

"She will need a calm environment." Mansell reached down to rub behind Ruby's ear.

Elizabeth looked disappointed. Darcy understood why. Her house was not calm. Not like his. Nor would her father appreciate the disruptive addition to his household. Darcy watched Ruby sniff his boots, her tail whipping against Elizabeth's skirts. Her deafness was merely a challenge to meet, a worthy one on which he already had formulated several ideas regarding her training.

But she was a Great Dane!

He pressed his eyes closed. Could he honestly say that all Great Danes were the same as the one that had bitten him? Was it fair to discredit the entire breed over the offense of one? He had been intolerant of her sort since his incident, but was he wrong to hold on to his resentment when it meant the life of the creature licking the toes of his boots? Between Ruby's contented innocence, Elizabeth's obvious distress, and Darcy's newfound determination to prove the warmth of his compassion, he contemplated what he never before would have considered.

"I will take Ruby with me to London this afternoon."

Mansell beamed. "That is very good of you, sir. Very kind."

Richard cast Darcy a knowing side-eye, which Darcy effectively ignored. He had eyes only for Elizabeth, who tilted her chin and looked at him with something akin to approval. A new look—a rather pleasant one which lasted longer than an eye blink this time—spread warmth through Darcy's chest.

It was a look he reflected on often over the course of the next hour as he faced Chalmers' barely restrained displeasure and Richard's sporadic outbursts of laughter. Darcy had made his decision, and he would commit himself fully to the task of seeing to Ruby's needs. Did that make him a swayable fool who would soon regret his responsibility? Almost certainly.

But if this act of good will forged the beginning of something Darcy could not yet see or anticipate, then he would be the happiest fool in England.

CHAPTER 8

With Colonel Fitzwilliam's attention arrested by the scene, Elizabeth was left free to watch Mr. Darcy as intently as she wished. He was more perceptive than she wanted to believe. It had not occurred to her that there was a physical hindrance to explain Ruby's behavior.

The puppy never looked up when anyone whistled or called to her, but when she focused her vision on a target, she was unswerving in her attention. All the clues had been there, and yet Elizabeth had not seen what Mr. Darcy had.

It made her wonder how he had missed seeing the clues of Jane's affection toward Mr. Bingley. Was it possible that there had not been enough clues to observe? After all, Charlotte had not noticed any particular attachment. When she had suggested that Jane ought to show Mr. Bingley more encouragement,

Elizabeth had laughed. The counsel seemed ridiculous, and she had said nothing to Jane.

She should have said something.

Not that Mr. Darcy was exempt from blame merely for admitting to his mistake or for having a modicum of justification. Elizabeth stiffened her spine at the thought. He had still been wrong to presume to interfere.

However, she could no longer look upon him without a more generous measure of respect. She had not believed him capable of humility, but not only had he apologized, he had honestly admitted to a deception which could not fail but cast him in an unfavorable light and for which he could have little hope of forgiveness. That, too, surprised her. He sought her forgiveness. She had assumed he considered her too low in his estimation to seek her good opinion.

Her thoughts returned to Ruby. Mr. Darcy had perceived the pup's need and had selflessly come to her aid. He would take exceptional care of her; of that, Elizabeth was certain. The man was not the sort to do anything half-heartedly. He took his responsibilities seriously, which might explain why Mr. Bingley accepted his advice as though it were divinely inspired. Their friendship was longstanding—similar to her friendship with Charlotte—and Mr. Bingley would have little reason to doubt Mr. Darcy's counsel. Oh, how she wished she had listened to Charlotte and that Mr. Bingley had ignored Mr. Darcy.

Elizabeth was perilously close to forgiving Mr. Darcy, so it was with dogged relief she welcomed the remembrance of another of his sins. What of the matter with Mr. Wickham? How could Mr. Darcy explain denying the man his rightful inheritance? Of cutting him off so mercilessly? When she had brought up the subject at the Netherfield Ball, Mr. Darcy's tone had fairly dripped with scorn. Resentment had hardened his features.

So consumed was Elizabeth in her thoughts, she hardly remembered when she had turned away from the kennel in the direction of the parsonage and was accompanied by Mr. Darcy and Colonel Fitzwilliam.

The former seemed content to stew on his own musings, while the colonel spoke enough for all three of them. She tried to give more attention to her more animated escort and to at least nod and smile on cue, but her gaze often wandered of its own volition to the stoic cousin who had given evidence of a softer heart than she had suspected him to possess.

Both Mr. Collins and Charlotte were out, and Elizabeth was able to retire to her room once the gentlemen had deposited her safely inside the parsonage. She watched them return to Rosings from the narrow opening between the wall and the curtain.

Mr. Darcy turned to look over his shoulder, straight at her. Elizabeth spun until her back rested against the wall beside the window, her breath coming in agitated heaves. Just as quickly, she rolled her eyes at herself for acting like a silly goose. She was free to look out of the window at whatever she pleased, and if Mr. Darcy happened to be part of the view, then so be it. She need not retreat as though she had something to hide.

Resuming her place at the window, she pulled aside the curtains. After Mr. Darcy departed, it was unlikely she would ever see him again.

Not a minute over an hour later, Darcy found himself sitting in his carriage across from Richard, Ruby's head growing heavy against his leg and a pool of her drool seeping into his breeches.

Chalmers and Richard's batman would follow behind them. Time was of the essence if Darcy meant to call on Bingley before nightfall. It was the height of the season, and he could not expect his sociable friend to be home after a certain hour.

He looked up to see Richard smirking at him. "I never thought I would see the day you would humble yourself for a young lady beneath your notice." He patted Ruby's head, earning a contented grunt from the puppy.

"The driver said she was too young to sit on the box with him," Darcy explained.

Richard's eyebrow arched. "I was speaking of another young lady."

Elizabeth. Darcy scowled. So far, his humility had

earned him a harsh scolding from his aunt Catherine for departing a day earlier than planned, he was now saddled with a dog he had no experience caring for, and his favorite travel breeches were ruined.

"I see she has you well-trained already." Richard guffawed.

Darcy tried to appreciate the humor in his situation, but levity eluded him. He was in no mood for riddles. "To which lady do you refer now?"

Richard shrugged. "Does it matter? Either one will serve the purpose."

"I will not allow you to compare Miss Elizabeth to a dog, Richard. If you mean to insult her, you can find another carriage to London."

Richard's eyebrows shot up toward his hair. "You defend the character of Miss Elizabeth when my jest was clearly intended for you? My God! You *are* smitten!"

Darcy could not deny it, so he retrieved the dull tome beside him and pretended to read.

CHAPTER 9

Darcy's mood soured with each successive tap on his carriage roof to signal the coachman that Ruby required a brief reprieve.

"We are making remarkably good time, considering we must stop every quarter of an hour," Richard commented dryly.

"Would you have her soil the interior?"

Richard held up his hands, palms out. "You mistake my meaning, Darcy. I am impressed by your consideration."

Darcy narrowed his eyes at his cousin. He had expected a jab, not praise, and he did not trust it.

"Yes, the last time I saw fit to travel at such a pace was when I accompanied my brother and his family from London to Matlock."

"You said you would never travel with them again."

Richard snorted. "You would have determined the

same had my little nephew burped sour milk all over your coat." He grinned at Ruby. "You would not do such a thing, now, would you, love? You are a good girl."

Ruby nudged his hand with her nose.

"She is a clever one, Darcy. She cannot hear me, and yet she understands I am pleased with her."

"She is not blind."

"I did not say she was. Lord, you are prickly today."

"We could have been in London by now." Darcy cast an accusatory glance at his new pet, who seemed to grin at him with her mouth open. It was impossible for him to remain cross at her, no matter how hard he tried. He smiled back, petting her when she nudged him.

"You did not have to ride in the coach, you know. You could have easily ridden ahead of the carriages," Richard pointed out.

"And leave Ruby with the coachman?"

Richard looked at him levelly. "Yes."

Darcy stopped himself before he discredited the idea vehemently. The fact was that he could have done precisely what Richard suggested, but he felt responsible for the animal and he would have fretted all the way into town unless he personally saw to her welfare.

They reached Mayfair and Brook Street late in the afternoon. Accompanying the carriage to the mews, Darcy made arrangements for Ruby to stay at the stable with the groom, knowing that neither his housekeeper nor his butler would appreciate being charged with an oversized puppy intent on chewing on everything within her reach.

"You mean to call at Bingley's immediately?" Richard stretched his limbs.

Darcy thought the reply was obvious. It was the reason for their early departure from Kent.

Richard clapped him on the shoulder. "I doubt he will be in, but please give my regards to Miss Bingley."

That gave Darcy pause. He had no desire to see Miss Bingley. She would assume his call was intended for her when nothing could be further from the truth. Perhaps he should try Bingley's club first.

"I will leave you to chase him over town tonight." Richard chuckled. "Shall we depart from your house at the usual time on the morrow? Allow Bingley a chance to wake at his leisure and break his fast?"

We? "I do not recall inviting you."

"No, you did not, but I would be remiss if I allowed an opportunity to watch you grovel pass me by."

"You are a pest."

"So I am often told. By you, usually. Everyone else considers me charming." Richard walked away, leaving Darcy to glare at his back and wonder yet again why they were friends.

With a sigh, he owned that, while Richard delighted in provoking him, he was a good man and a loyal ally who was completely trustworthy.

He was also quite often—quite maddeningly—

correct. Bingley was not at his club. Nor was he at his residence.

Miss Bingley must have instructed the butler to see Darcy in, for he had no sooner inquired if Bingley was there than he was being escorted upstairs to the parlor where his friend's sisters sat entertaining other guests. Miss Bingley preened and implied to all present that Darcy was calling on her, a lie he squelched before the gossip had a chance to start by immediately retiring.

Disgruntled, Darcy returned to the stables. There was nothing left to do but to call on Bingley on the morrow, just as Richard had foreseen.

The groom took off his hat and scratched his head. "Mr. Darcy, how fortuitous you returned so quickly." He wiped his brow and replaced his hat as though the last hour had been a trial.

Taking a deep breath, Darcy prepared himself for bad news. "Was she much trouble?"

"I doubt she meant to be, but the stables are no place for an untrained puppy. She has the funniest little bark. It was plain to me she was trying to call for you, but it agitated the horses. I had no option but to tie her up and send the stable boy to the house for a bone to occupy her. By the time the boy returned, the dog had chewed through the rope."

Darcy's heart lurched in his chest. "She is not lost, is she?"

"No, no. The little lass is safe. I put her inside the tack room. However, the horses are not too keen on her, and she startled the poor lad when he finally returned with her bone. I explained that she was after the bone, not him, but she is so large, almost as tall as the lad when she stood on her hind legs, I fear he remains unconvinced." The stable boy in question stood behind the groom at a respectful distance.

Addressing the boy, Darcy asked, "Are you hurt? Did she bite or scratch you?"

Stepping closer, the lad continued to keep a wary eye on the tack room opposite. "No, sir." His boldness increased as he passed the tack room. "I thought she was tied up, so it gave me a scare when I rounded the corner and she jumped up to nab the bone out of my hand. She lacks manners, but her nose is sound. She knew I was coming before she saw me."

The groom shot the boy a silencing look. The youth would get a proper scolding for being so free with his criticism, but Darcy would not allow it when he had merely spoken the truth. "She has much to learn yet, but I thank you for keeping her here and watching over her."

The groom doffed his hat again, passing it between his hands. "If it is all the same with you, Mr. Darcy, I will return her to your capable hands, unless..." He swallowed hard. "Unless, that is, you wish for her to... stay... here."

The concern on his brow made Darcy pinch back a laugh. "I will take her to the house lest she agitate your charges more than she already has."

"That suits us well, sir. Thank you." The groom exhaled audibly.

Cook was none too happy to receive the dog in the kitchen, as she had already forfeited her best soup bone for the "little mongrel." Aunt Catherine would have exchanged cross words at the implication that one of her dogs lacked the purest bloodlines, but Darcy understood Cook's meaning and reassured her that, although his soup at dinner would lack its usual flavor, he was grateful for her sacrifice on Ruby's behalf. This was received with several clucks and an improved opinion of the puppy, who sat like an angel on top of the toe of Darcy's boot as though she forbade him to move lest he leave her alone again.

After repeating the stew recipe Mansell had described, Darcy left Cook in a much-improved mood. Ruby padded alongside him up the carpeted stairs to his rooms. There was nowhere else for her. He would have to keep her with him.

She dozed by the fire while he saw to some awaiting correspondence. If she remained this quiet, it would not be too difficult of a night, although he would need to take her to the garden if she did wake. Chalmers retrieved some old blankets and expertly fashioned them into a cushioned mattress in the corner, which Ruby seemed to appreciate. She spun around several times, then settled in.

Three times between midnight and six o'clock, Darcy awoke to her whimpers and her warm body beside him on his bed. The first two times, he promptly took her outside, then returned her to her own bed. By the third time, Darcy was too tired to care where she slept so long as she allowed him to rest.

So he permitted her to lie at the foot of the bed… only for that night, of course.

CHAPTER 10

As with all things Darcy did not look forward to doing, he set about completing the odious task in the most expedient way possible.

Ruby did her best to hamper his progress. She was ever at his side, tripping him as he moved about his bedchamber and sending poor Chalmers into paroxysms every time she rubbed against Darcy's newly brushed breeches or licked his meticulously polished boots.

An hour later than Darcy had planned to depart, Richard breezed unannounced into the yellow breakfast parlor, where Darcy was doing his best to placate his agitated stomach with tea and dry toast. What was another half hour delay? With a resigned sigh, Darcy gestured at the sideboard. "Have you eaten?"

Setting a gold papered box with a satin bow

wrapped around it on the table, Richard grabbed a plate and served himself enough to feed two men.

Ruby squirmed at Darcy's side, distracted by a bird hopping on a tree branch on the other side of the window. Darcy tapped her gently on the back with two fingers to get her attention. Then, keeping his elbow down, he raised his palm to his shoulder. More out of habit than for her benefit, he firmly said, "Sit."

She licked the top of his boot, then tried to climb on to his lap.

"How is her training going?" Richard sat across from him, shoving the box he had set on the table off to the side.

Darcy sighed—he seemed to have an excess of them that morning. He had spent many restless hours the night prior pondering how best to communicate with Ruby. He had settled on hand signals. Something easy for Darcy and his household to remember and use, and distinct enough that the dog could see them from a distance without confusion.

His greatest difficulty was getting her attention. He tapped her back again and, when she looked at him, he repeated the palm-to-shoulder motion. "Sit." Another boot lick and a paw on his leg.

Richard smirked. "Is that what you have been teaching her? She is a very accomplished boot-licker."

Sensing Richard's merriment, their topic of discussion added her own howls and yips.

Tapping her back, Darcy raised his finger to his lips. "Shh."

Richard shook his head. "Now that is a gesture I remember well. We never heeded our nurses when they shushed us, either."

Ruby looked at Darcy adoringly, not knowing what he wanted but eager to please. A piece of his heart tugged. When she quieted down, he rewarded her with a bite of kipper and shot his cousin a scathing glare for criticizing his charge.

Draining the last of his tea, Darcy rose to call Bates. If he was going to leave the animal behind, he would have to ensure that his butler recalled the signs he had taught him earlier. Before he could take a step, Ruby wormed between his feet.

"Down." Darcy pressed his flat hand downward.

"You have really thought this through." Richard sounded impressed, though Darcy did not understand why. Everything he did was thoroughly thought through. Well, everything except offering to adopt a deaf Great Dane and undertake her training. That had been spontaneous and entirely driven by his desire to please Elizabeth (not that Richard needed to know that).

Feeling a distraction necessary, Darcy altered the course of their conversation. "More than I have thought about what to say to Bingley." He checked the time. "I really ought to be going. I do not suppose you are here to stay with Ruby?"

"When I can offer you my support at Bingley's? Not a chance, Darce. You are my cousin and my friend, and I will not desert you in your dark hour."

Darcy lowered his chin, his gaze fixed on Richard. "You wish to witness my humiliation when I apologize."

Richard shrugged. "You do not wish for my moral support?" He took a big bite, eyes glinting as he chewed.

Bates entered the parlor then. Over the next few minutes, Darcy repeated the signs he had determined to use for Ruby's training until Bates assured him they were branded in his memory.

To these, Richard added another—a raised thumb the archers of medieval times used to signal that they and their bows were in good condition and ready to fight. He suggested using the gesture to praise Ruby when she obeyed.

Darcy raised his thumb and smiled at the puppy. "Good girl," he said. Though Ruby could not know the meaning of the signal yet, she wiggled her bottom half happily.

Turning his attention back to Bates, he said, "Perhaps you could engage the assistance of another servant fond of dogs to keep her out of harm or entertained in the garden."

Bates nodded, no doubt relieved that he was not expected to have the dog underfoot for the rest of the morning. "I know just the person with whom to entrust Miss Ruby." Promising a prompt return, Bates excused himself.

Turning to Richard, who dabbed his lips with the napkin and pushed his chair back, Darcy suggested, "Shall we depart?"

"I am at your service, as always."

"I would rather you not be."

Richard grinned. "I do not doubt you mean that."

"And yet, you are still here."

"Moral support," Richard insisted with a wink.

"More like meddlesome obtrusion."

"Call it what you will, Darcy. I feel rotten for being the one to cast you in such an unfavorable light. Although, one could easily argue that it is to your favor that your crime—"

"It was hardly a crime," Darcy interrupted.

"I suppose that depends on from whose point of view you consider the matter."

Darcy felt his jaw clench. Richard was right. Elizabeth had made it plain that she saw him as the villain.

Having nobody to stop him, Richard yammered on. "Really, Darcy, you should thank me for bringing to light that which would have caused a breach between you and the entire Bennet family before an attachment was formed. Father always says that good communication is vital in a happy union."

"Blabbing gossip is not good communication."

Richard had sense enough to look contrite. "I will

own, I spoke out of turn. I am merely trying to help you see the positive side of this difficulty."

Darcy doubted his cousin's motive was as altruistic as he claimed, but Richard always had been one to dwell on opportunity and advantages. If he had gone to the continent, Darcy had no doubt his name would have been printed in the newspapers as often as General Wellesley's.

True to his word, Bates returned with a maid. "Sarah is one of Cook's helpers. Perhaps you recall the surname Higgins?"

Darcy looked closer at the maid. "Higgins? Was your father the kennel keeper at Pemberley?"

She bobbed a curtsy, her head bowed. "Yes, sir. My brothers stayed on at Pemberley, and I was offered a post here after his passing."

He remembered Higgins well. He was a good man, as tender and firm with his dogs as he was with his own children. If Darcy recollected correctly, there had been five children, and the maid standing before him would have been around twelve years of age when her father had died unexpectedly of a diseased heart. Darcy's father had immediately seen that his wife and children had sustenance and work. "I am sorry for your loss."

She looked up, her eyes bright. "It was a long time ago, sir." Her voice wavered.

"How long?"

"Ten years."

"It has been five years since my father died, and I still miss him. I doubt five years more will alter that."

"Thank you, sir," she said with a soft smile. Clearing her throat, she tapped Ruby on the back and held her arms out. "Mr. Bates said this means 'come.' Is this correct, sir?"

Ruby pranced over to the maid, sniffing her apron.

"Yes. You are familiar with the other signs?"

Bates said, "I will show her the rest once we get Miss Ruby out to the garden. If she is to be a frequent figure at Darcy House, I think it best to introduce her to the rest of the staff while she is still a... manageable... stature."

With a nod from Bates, Sarah smacked her hands against her apron and spun to run down the hall, Ruby bounding after her.

"Thank you, Bates. She is perfect."

Another bow of the head. "My pleasure, sir. Is there anything else you require?" Far from appearing put out, Bates seemed pleased.

"That is all, I thank you. I do not plan to tarry, but I am content in the knowledge that Ruby is in capable hands."

At that, Richard retrieved his box from the table and, together with Darcy, he walked out to the pavement. Bingley's house was a comfortable walking distance and the day was too fine to waste inside a carriage. Darcy understood why Elizabeth preferred to walk. He did too. He would much rather it was she beside him instead of his cousin.

Gesturing at the box cradled in the crook of Richard's arm, Darcy asked, "Have you turned your eye to Miss Bingley?"

Richard shivered. "Much too contentious for my taste. No, this is a peace offering—my contribution to your cause, in case Bingley is not in a forgiving mood."

Darcy frowned. "I have never known him not to be, and I hate being the one to test his limits." He eyed the box. "Macarons?"

"His favorite, directly from Greek Street."

Wavering between disapproval of what was essentially a bribe to curry Bingley's forgiveness and regret that he had not thought of it, Darcy continued silently down the pavement. The reality that he might lose his most amiable friend saddened Darcy, but he must prepare himself for the probability.

Richard glanced askance at him. "Not everyone's nature is as resentful as yours."

"Is this how you mean to show moral support—by criticizing my character? Would you prefer me to suffer fools?"

Raising his hand in protest, Richard said, "One question at a time, Darcy."

"Would you allow others to trample over my goodwill?" Darcy pressed, his agitation piqued at the dreaded task before him and his infernal cousin's constant quibbles when all Darcy had done was answer

Bingley's question as honestly as his convictions allowed. He had done nothing wrong!

"Never!"

"Then tell me why you call my nature resentful."

Richard considered long enough for Darcy to fix on the rhythm of their footfalls. "How many mistakes have you made in your lifetime?"

"You cannot answer a question with another question."

"Answer me, Darcy."

"Such a thing cannot be quantified. I hope I have not made many grave mistakes to the detriment of my household and those who depend on me, but nobody can escape mistakes in judgment or in trivial matters." *Really, what a question!*

"You refer to those serious mistakes which might cause injury to others besides you but which were unintentionally done as grave?"

Darcy looked about to ensure nobody could overhear their conversation, his scowl deepening. Speaking softly, he said, "I underestimated Wickham. And I hired Mrs. Younge on recommendation when I should have personally seen to a thorough investigation of her background. If you wish for me to enumerate my every fault—"

Richard interrupted. "It is not reasonable to peer into the past of every single servant."

"I should have done so for Georgie. She suffered from my failure, and to continue on as before would be an act of negligence."

"I cannot argue with you there. However, I will counter that Mrs. Younge's intentions were calculated, and therefore her example does not serve. I am speaking of someone who unintentionally acts in error. Such as yourself."

"I do not expect Bingley to forgive me. Were I in his position, I could not."

"Ha! There it is! Were you less resentful, you would react as most would—with forgiveness after a few hours, perhaps days even, of anger. Then you would move on and forget the whole affair."

Darcy gasped. "How? I find it difficult to believe that others can be so forgetful of the wrongs done against them."

"People who mean no harm—good people—make mistakes all the time. Does that make them unworthy?"

"It makes them untrustworthy."

"Even if they are repentant and make necessary amends?"

"That would improve them in my estimation, but how can trust be won once it is lost?"

Richard sighed. "I see this is a topic on which we shall find no accord."

"I pity you the harm you are bound to suffer for it, Rich."

"And I pity you the friendships you shall never enjoy, the enriching conversations of which you will deprive yourself, and the connection to the good of humanity of which you proudly deprive yourself."

They stood in front of Bingley's residence, and Darcy was relieved at the timeliness of their arrival. Never before had he found Richard's company so cumbersome.

CHAPTER 11

Bingley was in and delighted to receive them. He set aside his newspaper and sent for more coffee.

Darcy watched as his friend engaged Richard in idle chatter. He was paler than Darcy remembered him being at Netherfield Park; his collars seemed too large, too loose. His smile was as wide as usual, but there was something flat and dead in his eyes which suggested his manners were forced.

Richard set the gold box on the table in front of Bingley. "I took the liberty of bringing your favorites."

Bingley's smile widened, his eyes crinkling. "From Greek Street?"

"They are a favorite of my mother and sisters as well."

Plucking at the ribbon and untying the box, Bingley

sniffed the contents before he pushed it toward Darcy and Richard. "Do you care for some?"

Bingley's kindness worsened Darcy's guilt. He did not deserve it.

"Whatever is the matter, Darcy? Do you need more sugar for your coffee? I fear I might have used most of it." Bingley tilted the sugar basin toward him.

Recognizing that the longer he waited, the harder it would be, Darcy folded his hands together on top of the table and began. "I must apologize."

Bingley released his hold on the sugar bowl, sending the porcelain wobbling in circles.

Darcy reached out to steady it, continuing, "When you asked me if I believed an offer of marriage to Miss Bennet would be advisable, I gave you my opinion freely and according to the best of my understanding of the lady."

"Jane," Bingley whispered, blindly setting his macaron back inside the box.

Darcy forged ahead. "I was wrong about Miss Bennet. Miss Elizabeth told me in no uncertain terms that her sister was very much in love with you. She assured me that your departure from Hertfordshire broke Miss Bennet's heart as much as I suspect yours to be. I am sorry." Having spit out the words in one exhale, Darcy sucked in a much-needed breath of air.

Bingley furrowed his brow. "Sorry? For what? For answering the question I put to you?"

"For being wrong."

The furrow deepened. "Do not be stupid, Darcy. I am wrong all the time, which was why I asked for your opinion. You are steadier than I am."

Darcy leaned back. He had expected to be reprimanded, not excused. "But the things I said… the obstacles I mentioned…"

Bingley waved him off. "Her family's want of circumstance and propriety? You forget, Jane would have to endure Caroline and Louisa besides my uncles, who are still in trade. How could I hold her family's conduct against her when mine leaves much to be desired?"

Richard failed to hide a grin behind his cup. "What of her lack of a dowry?"

"I mean to marry for love, not a fortune."

"An enviable prospect," Richard grumbled good-naturedly.

Bingley nodded. "And one I do not intend to squander." He rubbed his hand through his hair. "Though that is precisely what I have done."

With a pointed look at Darcy, Richard said, "Not intentionally, surely."

Darcy returned his glare. He would apologize a dozen times over before he would admit to Richard that he had been right.

Oblivious to the altercation at his table, Bingley looked intently at Darcy. "You said Miss Elizabeth was your source of information?" More to himself than to anyone else, he added, "I suppose she would know better than anyone. Better even than you?"

Darcy nodded, the pressure building in his head. "I do not doubt her estimation. If she said her sister suffered at your departure, then it must be so."

The foolish grin spreading over Bingley's face vanished in a flash. "Wait. How did you come to speak of me and Jane to Miss Elizabeth?"

Sucking in a breath, Darcy pressed his fingers against his temples. "We had a disagreement." He ignored Richard's snort.

"About Jane and me?" Bingley asked, his face twisted in blatant confusion.

"She was staying at Hunsford parish as Mrs. Collins' guest while Richard and I were visiting my aunt at Rosings Park." The admission did nothing to ease the tension building in his head. Clasping his hands together, Darcy squeezed his knuckles until they turned white. "It has been many months since I have considered Miss Elizabeth the handsomest lady of my acquaintance in character as well as appearance." He had not meant to confess his attachment, and Darcy could only blame his admission on the foremost position his affection had placed in his thoughts.

Bingley's jaw dropped. "You called her 'tolerable enough' and refused to dance with her!" Then his face turned red. "You advised me against the eldest Bennet when you were developing a *tendre* for her sister? Darcy, how could you? That is—that is—"

"Hypocritical?" Richard supplied. "Duplicitous? High-handed? Perhaps diabolical? You have left out the best part, Darcy. You have not told Bingley—"

Darcy wished Richard would go to the devil, but he could not allow Bingley to hear his secret from anyone other than himself. "I intended to make her an offer of marriage."

Bingley stammered. "B-but why? Why, Darcy, blast you!?"

Darcy leaned against the back of his chair, feeling deflated. "I love her."

"And I love Jane!" Bingley rubbed his hands through his hair and over his face. "I would have married her in a heartbeat had you not told me you believed her indifferent."

"I was wrong."

Bingley groaned. "And, oh, how I have wronged her! My dearest Jane!"

Determined to clear himself of all of his faults, Darcy continued. "That is not all. Miss Bennet has been in London these past three months, at least."

Bingley's gaze pierced Darcy through. "And you knew this?" His voice boomed louder than Darcy had ever heard.

"I did, and I purposefully hid it from you."

"Did my sisters know?" Bingley's complexion was as white as his cravat.

"Miss Bennet called on them shortly after arriving in town. Of her call, I only recently learned from her sister. Had I known earlier, I would have had to reconsider my conviction of the lady's affection."

Covering his face with his hands, Bingley sat quietly for some time. When he finally dropped them, he spoke. "What that dear lady must have suffered at my hand. How could I ever secure her forgiveness? Worse still, her heart? She must abhor me, and rightly so. I rather hate myself right now."

Richard pushed the box of pastries closer. "Do not be so harsh on yourself, Bingley. Have a macaron."

Bingley dropped his head into his hands, elbows leaning against the table. "You have never been in love, Richard. Do you have any idea how wretched it feels to have caused pain to the one person in the world I would swear to protect and cherish and love above all others?" He turned to Darcy. "I apologize for my manners. Please accept my congratulations on your upcoming nuptials."

A dagger to the gut. Darcy grunted, "I did not propose."

"I do not understand. You said you intended to make an offer, and I have never known you not to follow through on your chosen course."

Darcy grimaced. Must he be repeatedly humiliated? "I went to the parsonage with every intention of making an offer, but I was… interrupted."

Richard nudged Bingley's arm. "You will have to call at Darcy House to meet the 'interruption.'"

Darcy took a deep breath, speaking from between

gritted teeth. "A story for another time. What I came to do today was admit to my error so that reparations might be made. Miss Bennet is still in town. She is currently residing with her uncle on Gracechurch Street."

Bingley hopped to his feet. "I shall call on her at once!" Plucking a macaron from the box, he pointed his pastry-wielding hand at Darcy. As quickly as his boldness had roused Bingley to action, his decisiveness wavered, and he lowered the macaron. "Unless you think I ought to wait?"

Darcy kept his mouth shut. He was done interfering, although he could not help but think that if Bingley wished to be the master of his own happiness, he would do well to make his own decisions.

Popping the macaron in his mouth and chewing slowly, Bingley sat back down. "Pray do not answer that. I should not have expected you to make such an important decision for me in the first place. It is my weakness, and it is obvious to me now how ill it has served me." He rubbed his hands over his face and reached for another macaron. "I envy your decisiveness, Darcy. Had I been firmer in my own convictions, I would not have relied so heavily on yours. I should have risked a refusal to learn her true feelings."

While Darcy applauded his friend's newfound resolve, he could not help but recall Elizabeth's concerns. "Are you decided on Miss Bennet? Any young lady deserves a gentleman's wholehearted dedication."

"I miss Jane more now than when I first departed from Hertfordshire. Everything reminds me of her, and I would live the rest of my days in regret if I did not beg for her forgiveness. I will grovel on my knees if it means she will grant me a second chance."

Richard stirred the last of the sugar into his coffee. "You are not angry with Darcy?"

Bingley looked between Richard and Darcy, finally suspecting the undercurrent of their previous altercation. "I do not know what you two are about, and I pray you do not muddle my mind further by telling me. Of course I am angry." He crossed his arms over his chest and lowered his chin. "But I am angrier at myself for allowing myself to be persuaded." He looked over Darcy's shoulder, his eyes narrowing into slits. "At least you admitted to your error, which is more than I can say for my spiteful, conniving sisters."

Darcy was grateful not to be the recipient of Bingley's ire, but he was not entirely at ease. He had gotten off too easily and felt impending punishment must be lurking around the corner.

WHILE RICHARD WOULD HAVE PREFERRED for Bingley to make Darcy suffer a bit more, he also recognized a valuable ally when he saw one.

When it was time to depart, he stood but tarried until Darcy had vacated the room. Motioning at the box of macarons, he noted, "You had best hide those before your sisters see them."

Bingley's eyes doubled. He snatched the box, cradling it against his chest. "On my honor, they shall not taste one bite!" His cheeks bloomed with color and his eyes brightened. "Do you think—?" He bit his tongue and shook his head. "I shall go by Greek Street before I attempt to call on Jane. If she is unwilling to receive my call, at least she can try these delicious macarons. She would enjoy sharing them with her relatives. She has a generous nature."

Richard squeezed Bingley's shoulder. He would do well. "As do you, Bingley. Continue in this course, and you shall make a fine husband."

"If Jane will have me. I dare not presume."

How opposite Bingley and Darcy were! Richard shook his head in wonder, then snapped out of his reverie.

Glancing at the doorway and knowing Darcy would be pacing impatiently on the other side, Richard dropped his voice and stated, "Darcy is in need of our help."

"What has happened? How may I assist?" Bingley moved toward the door, and Richard caught him before he got too far.

"He is in dire need of help, only he does not know it," Richard hissed.

Bingley's eyebrows knit together. "I do not understand. You need aid to help Darcy? He never needs help!"

Richard heard Darcy clear his throat out in the entrance hall. "I shall explain later, but you may trust me on this. When it comes to affairs of the heart, Darcy is woefully incompetent. If we do not assist him, he will ruin his chances with Miss Elizabeth… if he has not already done so."

Eager to prove himself a man of action, Bingley extended his hand, and they shook on it. "Whatever it takes, I am at your command."

"Good. Because if my plan is to work, we will need to enlist Miss Bennet's help."

CHAPTER 12

Elizabeth returned to the cottage from a walk feeling as restless as she had at its start.

Five days had passed since the colonel and Mr. Darcy's departure, and Charlotte was often too busy to accompany Elizabeth for her long walks over the beautiful grounds. Elizabeth missed Colonel Fitzwilliam's conversation. He was charming and witty, and she appreciated his humor.

It was a convincing argument... until she realized how she held her breath around every bend, bridge, and byway. At every place her path had crossed Mr. Darcy's.

Either she was—dare she say it?—eager to see Mr. Darcy again, or she was anxious to avoid him. It must be the latter. It simply had to be. He was such a provoking individual, so high-handed and presumptuous! A more disagreeable man, Elizabeth would be hard-pressed to encounter.

Yet, there was a kindness to him.

It did occur to her that, after their conversation, he might attempt to clear the matter with Mr. Bingley, but Elizabeth quickly stifled the hope. Why would Mr. Darcy interfere on Jane's behalf when he believed her family too far beneath Mr. Bingley's notice?

Upon straightening her hair and washing up, Elizabeth joined Charlotte in her friend's "particular" parlor. Mr. Collins was outdoors pruning his beloved rose bushes—an activity that Charlotte encouraged him to indulge. Charlotte was the picture of an industrious wife, sitting beside the window with her embroidery. "Did you have a pleasant walk?"

Elizabeth sat in the chair opposite. "You should have joined me. I would have enjoyed your companionship."

Pinching her lips together briefly, Charlotte looked up at Elizabeth with an arched brow. "In the absence of Mr. Darcy or Colonel Fitzwilliam's company, you mean?" Elizabeth opened her mouth to deny it, but Charlotte spoke before she could. "There was a letter for you in the post."

How strange! Elizabeth's family knew she was to depart from Hunsford in only three days. She would have expected whatever news they had to share would be sent to her uncle's address at Gracechurch Street.

That they risked the post missing her altogether gave cause for concern. "I hope all is well."

Fishing the letter from her apron pocket, Charlotte handed Elizabeth the sealed envelope. "It is in Jane's writing."

Elizabeth took the letter, her alarm growing. Tearing the paper in her haste to break the seal, she devoured the first line and heaved a sigh of relief when she saw Jane's opening words: *My Dearest Lizzy, I am so happy!*

Dropping her hand to her lap, she assured Charlotte. "All is well. Jane bears good news."

Her friend attended to her embroidery while Elizabeth read. Jane's letter was so conversational in tone, Elizabeth imagined Jane's excited voice and saw her dear sister's cheeks brightened with pleasure. *Mr. Bingley had no idea I was in town! Oh, Lizzy, can you believe it?*

The next sentence made Elizabeth stop and read it twice over. *Apparently it was Mr. Darcy who informed him of my presence. (I know you are determined to think poorly of the gentleman, but on this point, Mr. Bingley was firm. His source was none other than Mr. Darcy.)*

Elizabeth clutched the letter to her breast. Could it be that she had misjudged him yet again? She pored over the next lines, hungry for Jane's happy news.

Mr. Bingley immediately set out to present his card to Uncle, and he has since dined with us at Gracechurch. The children adore him, and Aunt commented that he is every-

thing a gentleman ought to be. Uncle is more reserved in his praise, but I can tell he is inclined to approve of Mr. Bingley.

And, Lizzy, he apologized for abandoning Netherfield Park so quickly and without so much as a farewell. His manners being so repentant, I could not withhold forgiveness. He begged my pardon many times over for the hurt he caused me.

You see, he believed me indifferent! I know I am modest by nature, but you would have been appalled at my boldness at that moment. He is confident where he stands in my estimation now. While I would never presume before, I am now hopeful.

Elizabeth read this final paragraph aloud. "It is about time!" Charlotte stabbed her needle through the linen. "I feared she had lost him when he left Hertfordshire."

"She so nearly did," Elizabeth said softly. Had it not been for her argument with Mr. Darcy five days prior, Jane would be melancholy still.

"You look pensive, Lizzy. Are you well?" Charlotte set her needlework aside.

Having nobody else to confide in and trusting her friend implicitly, Elizabeth described her confrontation with Mr. Darcy—about her charges and his justifications, about her accusations and his apology.

Charlotte's grin bewildered Elizabeth. "An interesting and rather suggestive development, indeed!"

Elizabeth gasped. "Suggestive of what?"

Reaching for her embroidery hoop, Charlotte

resumed stabbing the fabric. "As you are disinclined to believe what I tell you, I am determined not to speak a word on the subject."

"You tease! I admit you were correct to admonish me about Jane—"

"You laughed at me and said nothing at all of my concerns to your sister. I do not know why I waste my breath on you."

Elizabeth summoned a respectable degree of penitence. "You were right where I was wrong, and I am sorry."

Charlotte pinched her lips together, though Elizabeth could not discern with certainty whether she did so to appear more self-righteous or to hold back her laughter. "The unassailable Lizzy Bennet admitting she was wrong? How did that taste crossing your tongue?"

"Horrible! And you are wicked for reveling in it."

"Indulge me for a moment longer. Such occurrences are rare and must be reveled in properly."

Elizabeth rolled her eyes and chuckled. "Does Mr. Collins know this side of your character?"

Sitting taller in her chair, Charlotte appeared as stoic as a statue. "I will always choose harmony in my household over the satisfaction of having the last laugh or the final word."

Elizabeth could not imagine a duller existence. "I could never make such a sacrifice."

"No, I do not believe you could." Lowering her hoop to her lap, Charlotte fixed her gaze on Elizabeth. "Nor would you appreciate a husband who offered you little intellectual challenge."

High praise, indeed! And from a trusted friend who never uttered an insincere word. Unfortunately, she continued, "Nor would it be good for your character to always get your way."

"If you were not my dearest friend, I would be offended," Elizabeth grumbled.

Shaking her head, Charlotte smiled. "I am a weak creature, and I am finding it impossible to stick to my resolve that I would keep my suspicion to myself."

"I will listen with an open mind."

"I do not doubt you mean that."

Elizabeth turned toward the window, feeling her friend's chastisement. Once the sting died down, she asked, "Do you consider me narrow-minded?"

Charlotte pondered the question for a total of seven stitches. "In most things, no. But you are very certain in your opinions once you determine them, and for this I do not think you will care for what I shall tell you."

Elizabeth raised her chin, determined to prove Charlotte wrong.

"Very well," Charlotte said with a glint in her eye. "I believe that Mr. Darcy finds you more than tolerable. I am convinced that he likes you very much and that, given the chance, he would make you an offer of marriage."

Elizabeth choked back her laughter before it escaped.

Charlotte raised an eyebrow. "How can you explain his frequent calls during his stay here?"

"He was being polite!"

"I recall you complaining of his rudeness. Has your opinion changed?"

"He has been exceedingly rude to me and to my family, but he is not an absolute brute."

"He called every day." Charlotte looked positively smug.

"So did Colonel Fitzwilliam, and yet you do not suspect him of romantic notions."

"You and I both know he is not in a position to fall in love with you. Mr. Darcy, on the other hand—"

"Preposterous!"

"Is it? Were you aware that when you stayed in with a headache, Mr. Darcy did not even bother to appear? Her Ladyship was terribly put out."

Elizabeth was well aware of that detail, though she said nothing of it to Charlotte. She still could not fathom why Mr. Darcy had shown up at night at the parsonage when he knew she was alone. "He is too lofty—too proud to notice me."

Charlotte leaned forward. "And yet he spoke to Mr. Bingley. Why would he do that unless he sought your favor?"

"For his friend's benefit, surely!"

"And why did he relieve Mr. Mansell of the deaf puppy he did not have the heart to dispose of?"

"He is not completely without heart. Mr. Darcy

understood Ruby's predicament, and he kindly offered to take on her training and give her his protection."

Tilting her chin, Charlotte asked, "Now you are defending him? How extraordinary!"

Elizabeth scowled. "I am not as close-minded as you claim me to be."

"And you are not as indifferent to Mr. Darcy as you believe yourself to be."

Before Elizabeth could refute her friend's claim with a scathing retort, Mr. Collins stepped inside the parlor. "Forgive me, but I was walking past and I could not help but overhear your comment, my dear." He turned to his cousin and wiped his brow with a handkerchief. "Cousin Elizabeth, I must beg you not consider Mr. Darcy to be an appropriate match for one such as yourself when—"

Intervening before his plea stretched into a sermon, Elizabeth held up her hands. "Allow me to reassure you that no such thought had entered my mind."

Fumbling his handkerchief in his hands, Mr. Collins sighed. "I am glad to hear it. Mr. Darcy is engaged to his cousin Miss de Bourgh, and Lady Catherine would be most displeased to have her arrangement changed. Knowing you to be my relative would cause no end of conflict in our household were such a preposterous pairing to occur. Her Ladyship would be certain to make her displeasure felt."

He would no doubt have carried on longer had

Charlotte not intervened. "Shall I call for tea while you wash up?"

Mr. Collins looked at his hands, his shirtsleeves rolled up to his elbows and his nails encrusted with dirt. "Yes, of course. You are always so thoughtful and proper, my dear."

Once he had moved out of the room, Charlotte cast a calculating glance at Elizabeth. "Miss de Bourgh has no desire to marry her cousin."

Elizabeth smoothed her skirts, irritated with the flutter of glee she felt at Charlotte's information. Dismissing the unwanted emotion with a shrug, Elizabeth clasped her hands together and said flippantly, "Mr. Darcy may marry whomsoever he pleases. It hardly signifies to me."

Her friend smiled softly and returned to her needlework. After a few moments of uncomfortable silence where every flinch and shifting of her weight seemed to confirm Charlotte's outrageous opinion, Elizabeth decided that there was no time like the present to reply to Jane's letter

CHAPTER 13

Darcy tightened his grip on the leash as yet another gaggle of females attempted to stop him and admire his "adorable puppy."

"Tell me again how this is good for Ruby?" he grumbled to Richard and Bingley.

Richard smiled widely at the ladies, his hat settled at a rakish angle. "Had I known this pup would attract so many eligible ladies, I would have convinced you to continue her training in the park much sooner."

Bingley tipped his hat and continued searching for someone in the crowds. Darcy suspected that the reason his friend had persuaded him to join them at Hyde Park's walking path had nothing to do with Ruby's training and everything to do with Miss Jane Bennet. Bingley had been a frequent caller at the Gardiners' residence over the past two weeks.

Darcy knew it was foolish, but he found himself scanning over the crowds of pedestrians for Elizabeth.

Another lady cooed at Ruby and batted her eyelashes at the gentlemen as she passed. Darcy clenched his jaw. This was becoming insufferable. (For him. Richard lapped it up like a tomcat with a bowl of cream.)

Bingley, temporarily satisfied he was not missing Miss Bennet's company, added to the conversation. "The sooner Ruby becomes accustomed to being around other people and animals, the sooner you will be able to trust her to behave around them."

"But why here? The park is always crowded, but it is unbearable on a fine day such as this." Darcy turned, ready to walk back to his house.

Both Richard and Bingley grabbed his arms and turned him back, making him trip over the lead. They exchanged glances—duplicitous scoundrels that they were. Their presence in the park and Bingley's insistence that they walk across to the north-west enclosure had nothing to do with puppy training. Darcy was certain of it.

"Colonel Fitzwilliam!" greeted a man across the path.

Darcy stumbled to the side, nearly trampling Ruby and Bingley to widen the distance between himself and a full-grown Great Dane as tall as Darcy's elbow who accompanied the saluting officer coming near them. Georgiana's childhood pony was smaller!

"Oy, Darcy," complained Bingley, "how can you continue to fear the noble breed when that is what you can expect Ruby to become?" He gestured at the giant, who now glared at Darcy with dark, cold eyes. An ear-splitting bark rumbled through Darcy, making his limbs tremble and earning the dog a warning from his master.

"I apologize for Augustus. He only barks when he senses danger or fear. Aside from their throaty bark, Great Danes are known for being protective," the officer explained to Richard.

Casting a look over his shoulder at Darcy, who did his best to look unaffected now that his initial panic had subsided enough to control, Richard turned his acquaintance away, allowing Darcy and Bingley to continue down the path and away from Augustus the Great. There was an empty patch of grass near the Serpentine, and that was where Darcy directed their pack.

Richard joined them shortly. "That is General Sanders. He expressed an interest in Ruby for Augustus."

"She is three months old!" Darcy exclaimed, his disgust piqued at the thought of his little Ruby receiving the attentions of that colossal brute.

Tapping Ruby on the back, he went through the few signals he and all of his household—all of whom affectionately called her Miss Ruby—had been diligently practicing with her. Darcy raised his palm to his shoulder, and Ruby sat at his feet.

He flipped his thumb up, then plucked a bite of bacon from the napkin in his pocket.

"That was why the Dane barked at you!" Richard chuckled. "He smelled what you had in your pockets and was asking for a piece."

Ignoring him, Darcy stepped away as far as the lead allowed and opened his arms. "Come." He still found himself saying the commands aloud out of habit.

Ruby stood and cocked her head to the side as though to ask, *And where am I supposed to go?* She was only a couple of feet away.

Rubbing her favorite spot on her neck, Darcy shoved the leash into Bingley's hands. "If you insist on dragging me here for your own devices, you can make yourself useful." Signing to Ruby, Darcy commanded her to sit. He walked a few paces away. "When I signal her to come, drop the leash. Then repeat the command so she comes to you." Ruby performed beautifully. As did Bingley, who doled out praise generously when she returned to him.

Down by the lake, a boy and his nurse tossed bread crumbs to a group of geese. Richard warned them, "Pray take care. It is nesting season, and geese do not take kindly to intruders in their territory."

The nurse thanked him and promptly handed the boy another piece of bread, moving closer to the water's edge in complete disregard for Richard's warning.

Richard shook his head. "Some people must learn the hard way."

Bingley had yet to reach down for Ruby's leash. He was too busy searching the crowds walking along the broad footpath. Richard hissed at him, widening his eyes and twitching his head in Darcy's direction.

Darcy narrowed his eyes at them. That the two had hatched some ill-conceived plan against him was certain. From experience, Darcy knew that the surest way to find out what was going on was to feign complete disinterest. Bingley could not keep a secret or effect a bluff to save his life. And Richard, while a strategic whist player, always overplayed his hand.

Waving his arms to get Ruby's attention, Darcy heard the hisses by the lake at the same time he saw his furry student fix on the source of the commotion. He could not compete with a dozen flapping wings. The flying feathers and charging geese were too tempting a sight for a curious puppy. Ruby bolted toward the action. Too late, Darcy lunged for her leash and came up with a handful of grass.

"I thought she was a boar-hunter!" called Bingley, chasing after her.

Richard joined them, bounding toward the terrified boy and nurse. "Apparently she favors geese too!"

"Can't say I blame her. I rather favor goose, too. On my table." Bingley held his hands out in front of him, trying to place himself between the boy and the feathered furies.

"Blasted aggressive creatures." Richard faced the geese, adding to Bingley's barrier.

The nurse and child scampered away with hasty thanks, leaving a mob of angry, agitated waterfowl in their wake. In the middle of the pack was Ruby, barking and yipping at this wonderful game.

Darcy plunged into the middle just as a fiendish fowl nipped at Ruby's ear with its serrated beak. She yelped, and Darcy reached blindly through the blizzard of bird feathers, shoving his way inside the gang of provoked poultry to save her.

CHAPTER 14

Elizabeth wrapped her arm around her sister's. "This was a brilliant idea, Jane."

The setting was perfect. Their young cousins ran circles around Aunt and Uncle Gardiner along the park wall. The keeper's lodge provided a charming contrast to the noble Kensington Gardens on the opposite side, and a fence by the Serpentine River divided them from horses and carriages. On this side of the fence, the pastoral setting allowed for cows, from which the keeper made his famous cheesecake and syllabub to sell at his cake house.

Looking over the clusters of people milling about, Jane said absently, "They hardly needed convincing."

Elizabeth squeezed Jane's arm to her side. "How convenient for you. I do not suppose we might see Mr. Bingley, do you?"

Jane's blush was reply enough. "He did say he

planned to walk here this afternoon if the weather was fine."

"As I suspected," Elizabeth teased. "Do not be embarrassed, Jane. Should you *not* wish to spend more time with him, then I would have to take back my words and admit to Mr. Darcy that you are indifferent." She shook her head and laughed. "And that, I cannot allow."

Jane patted Elizabeth's hand and smiled softly. "I hope you do not hold his mistake against him. It was made in earnest, and I cannot fault him for attempting to protect his friend's happiness as eagerly as you protect mine."

"Fear not, sweet, forgiving Jane, I harbor no animosity toward the gentleman… regarding you." There was still the matter concerning Mr. Wickham to contend with, but Elizabeth could not deny that her estimation of Mr. Darcy had improved upon receiving Jane's letter.

Was Mr. Darcy still in London? Elizabeth had hoped to see him. Of course, he had little incentive to seek out her company after the tongue-lashing she had given him at Rosings. Still, he had acted honorably on Jane's behalf, and Elizabeth wanted to thank him. And see Ruby. She was curious to know how he and his new charge were getting on.

Jane dropped her arm and stepped away to look at Elizabeth. "Are you well? It is not like you to sigh so much, Lizzy."

Elizabeth had not realized her thoughts had altered her breath, making her regret apparent to her sister. Unwilling to dampen the glory of the day, Elizabeth tilted her head back until she felt the sun warming her cheeks. "The weather is perfect, and I am frustrated that I cannot remove my bonnet to take full advantage of it."

"Is that all?" Jane's tone expressed disbelief.

Not wishing to lie to her sister, Elizabeth said, "Mostly." If she considered the matter further, that proportion was not entirely accurate. Mr. Darcy provoked many more sighs than the weather, but Jane knew mathematics had never been Elizabeth's strength, so it was not a blatant falsehood.

Looking around for a change of topic, Elizabeth saw her youngest cousin running closer to the Serpentine. She called after him. "Be mindful of the geese, Henry!"

Uncle gave chase, reaching his son before he got too near the water's edge. "It is nesting season, and this is their home. They will not take kindly to curious little boys who trample too close to their eggs."

Little Henry's lip pooched out. "I saved my breakfast roll for them." He reached into his pocket, his frown deepening when he pulled out a handful of crumbs.

"Is that how you ate so quickly?" Aunt gasped. Seeing his eyes filled with tears, she tried to control her merriment at her son's sweet but ill-calculated gesture.

Emily, ever the caring eldest sister, wrapped her arm around her brother's narrow shoulders. "Do not cry, Henry. You can have another roll when we return home."

James, the middle child, crossed his arms. "Not mine! Mama says I am a growing boy and will be as tall as Papa if I do not skip meals."

Emily made a face at him. "Nobody threatened to take your food away from you. Henry may have my roll."

Aunt leaned closer to Jane and Elizabeth. "One would think that we suffer from a shortage of bread in the house."

Uncle had directed them farther up the path, nearer the keeper's garden. Two rows of trees lined two springs. A woman sat at a table covered with a red checkered tablecloth with glasses on top and chairs surrounding her stand. A servant jogged past them carrying a jug, which he handed to the woman.

Elizabeth looked over her shoulder to see a carriage waiting on the other side of the fence. The woman filled the jug, accepted her payment, and the servant ran back to the waiting carriage. As soon as the conveyance departed, another carriage took its place, this time, a child running to the woman selling spring water, his parents watching from the windows of their carriage.

"Have you tried the mineral water before?" Uncle

asked, a glint in his eye that Elizabeth did not quite trust.

Aunt's reply confirmed her growing skepticism. "It is touted to be a restorative without equal and highly salubrious."

In Elizabeth's experience, the food and drink described as most wholesome were often the least appetizing. But Uncle was already on his way to the water seller. He purchased seven glasses, and they each took one. Elizabeth downed hers down in three gulps, swallowing hard several times more to keep the liquid down. It was vile!

Emily did her best to imitate Jane, who delicately sipped from her glass and tried not to twist her face. The boys fared poorly. Henry stuck out his tongue and refused to drink after his first taste. James bravely persisted when Uncle told him that the mineral water from that very stream was a regular part of his diet when he was a young man, and to which he credited his healthy constitution and height (which was, truth be told, only slightly above that of the average gentleman; certainly not as tall as Mr. Darcy). Aunt and Uncle choked down the dreadful drink between chortles. Elizabeth, having been the first to finish, refused the offer of a refilled glass from the woman behind the table.

She occupied herself by looking about. At the second stream, she observed several people bathing their eyes with the crystal-clear water. She imagined that stream would taste much better than the horrible liquid they had just imbibed.

Once they had all emptied their glasses (with the exception of Henry, who happily gave the last of his to James since his brother was eager to be the taller of the two), Uncle suggested they make a brief stop at the cake house for cheesecake and syllabub. This suggestion was met with cheers, heightened by Aunt's foresight in bringing a blanket so that they might spread it over the grass and enjoy an outdoor picnic. Cheered with good company, children's laughter, delicious sugared treats, and warm sunshine, they chased off the remnants of the bitter tasting mineral water, and their spirits soared.

Jane still watched for Mr. Bingley, her disappointment only visible to those who knew her best as they slipped past the fence and walked along the path to Uncle's carriage. Shouts and high-pitched barks by the Serpentine drew several looks, theirs included. Elizabeth quickened her pace to get a better look. There was something familiar...

Elizabeth's jaw dropped.

Mr. Darcy was engaged in a scuffle against half a dozen geese at the edge of the lake. Ruby, no doubt trying to be helpful, barked and nipped at the hissing fowls, who flailed their wings and lashed at them with thick beaks. Mr. Bingley and Colonel Fitzwilliam attempted to distract the gaggle away from Mr. Darcy with no success. If only the two men would pull Ruby away, Mr. Darcy would follow. Did they not see that he only meant to protect her?

If she could get Ruby's attention, she could call her over. Waving her arms as she neared, it was not the dog's attention she secured. Mr. Darcy peeked over the arms protecting his face. "Miss Elizabeth!" He stepped backward, only to have his foot slip out from under him in the muddy bank. His maneuvers to right himself would have made the most talented ice skater envious, but between Ruby splashing into the lake after him and the shouts of the geese, he landed with an inelegant plunge in the murky water. Ruby took full advantage of his lowered height to lick his cheeks.

The sight of the great Fitzwilliam Darcy sitting shoulder-deep in the Serpentine was enough to send Elizabeth into stitches, but she contained her laughter. Colonel Fitzwilliam, on the other hand, did not bother to conceal his glee. By then, Mr. Bingley had found Jane and did not seem to notice anything except her.

Elizabeth held her breath and bit her cheeks, but when Mr. Darcy stood and resignedly plucked off the water grass from his shirt, Elizabeth could hold her mirth no longer. That was when Ruby finally noticed her. The puppy lunged out of the water, shaking her coat and spraying Elizabeth with dog-scented lake water.

"My apologies, Miss Elizabeth!" Mr. Darcy's face was a shade of red Elizabeth had never before seen. He reached for Ruby's leash to pull her away, but the excited canine dove into Elizabeth's skirts.

"My deepest apologies," he repeated.

Elizabeth's laughter deepened. What else could she do when his embarrassment was so plain and her skirts were drenched?

Spinning to the side to grab Ruby, Mr. Darcy dove for his dog's lead at the same time Elizabeth did from the opposite direction. Their heads crashed together with a jarring crack.

"Again, I apologize." He rubbed his forehead.

Elizabeth rubbed her head, too. "For having a hard head? Really, Mr. Darcy, I could have told you that without you offering proof." She bit her tongue as soon as the words flew over her tongue. She had wanted an opportunity to thank him, not to insult the man.

Except he laughed! Reaching for Ruby again, he caught the leash, but the miscreant ran around Elizabeth, the lead wrapping around her knees and pulling them together.

"Drop the leash!" Elizabeth exclaimed, her body crashing against Mr. Darcy's chest. His arms circled around her as, once again, he fought to right not only himself but to prevent her from tumbling to the ground. She felt the sinews of his muscles swell and strain, felt the solidity of his chest, felt his warmth, and smelled the sandalwood in his soap.

Straightening, Mr. Darcy made a gesture Elizabeth was too close to see and commanded, "Sit."

The line tugging Elizabeth's legs into Mr. Darcy's slackened, and she was able to step away from the gentleman to look at Ruby sitting obediently.

Elizabeth envied the animal's calm. Her own pulse raced and her cheeks burned. It had nothing to do with nearly falling and everything to do with Mr. Darcy's nearness and his hand cradling her elbow.

CHAPTER 15

A gentleman and his wife descended upon them, followed by three children. Elizabeth's London relatives. The shock on their faces proclaimed them as such.

Too late, Darcy dropped his hand from Elizabeth's elbow and stepped away, searching the ground at his feet for an explanation, although the feel of her in his arms lingered.

Had they seen him embrace her? Darcy looked about, a chill seizing him as he realized just how many people must have observed them.

Could he have acted differently? She might have been injured had he allowed her to fall.

He looked down at Ruby, who looked up at him adoringly. She would be the ruin of him. He ought to be angry, but how could he punish the puppy when she did not know the dangers of geese and had so much yet to learn? And especially when he would hand her the last of his soggy bacon as a reward for shoving Elizabeth into his arms? She wiggled her tail and barked at his pocket, waiting for her prize—seemingly reading Darcy's mind. He knew he ought not to reward her rambunctious behavior, but in the end, emotion won over rational thought. She did not mind that the rest of the bacon was wet and gobbled it down hungrily, licking Darcy's fingers for every last tasty morsel.

Richard must have decided to make himself useful, for he finally approached. Darcy glowered at him. Had his cousin come to his aid earlier, he would not have embraced Elizabeth publicly. "Where were you?" He shoved the leash into Richard's hands to ring out some of the water dripping from his cravat and coattails. Poor Chalmers. What he had to put up with lately…

Richard beamed at the dog as he leaned closer to Darcy and whispered, "Are you rewarding Ruby for sitting so prettily or for her role in your public display? Shall I congratulate you on your upcoming nuptials?"

Bingley, with Miss Bennet on his arm, joined the couple and their children and performed introductions. Mr. and Mrs. Gardiner regarded Darcy, and he did his best not to shrivel under their inspection. There was a glint of humor in their eyes, but he had not forgotten the shock he had seen on their faces earlier.

"Mr. Gardiner, I am sorry for the scene you witnessed." Darcy bowed his head, feeling as remorseful and humble as he had the one time he had given into temptation and his father had caught him skipping his Latin lessons to ride over the fields with his cousins.

"Such a tender scene," Richard murmured under his breath. Darcy shot him a look meant to silence him. He would not allow his cousin to make light of this, and certainly not in front of the man responsible for his nieces' reputations.

Mr. Gardiner shook his head, his expression neither agitated nor amiable. "My carriage is nearby. Might I suggest you allow me to convey you to your residence, Mr. Darcy? Mr. Bingley informs me it is not far."

Darcy wanted to refuse, and he might have done so had he not shifted his weight and heard his ruined boots squish and felt the seams in his breeches strain. Darcy House was not far, but he could not risk that kind of exposure. To refuse Mr. Gardiner's offer would be to make a spectacle of himself. "Thank you, sir. I find myself both grateful for your generosity and unable to refuse, though I regret the damage to your carriage squabs."

Mrs. Gardiner smiled. "We are a family with small children, Mr. Darcy. You cannot possibly do more damage to our conveyance than James and Henry have."

One of the boys, the taller one, scowled at his mother, while the smaller one grinned cheekily. The taller one returned his attention to Mr. Darcy, his chin tilted as though he were attempting to see the top of Darcy's head. "You must have drunk a lot of mineral water. And eaten lots of vegetables."

His parents' looks turned from contemplative to pleading in an instant. Understanding their struggle—for Darcy's own father had uttered the same nonsense about the importance of eating one's vegetables—he bent down to the boy. "I credit my height to Brussels sprouts."

The boy's mouth twisted. The poor lad must have similar taste to Darcy, who still winced inwardly whenever the dreaded vegetable appeared and had ordered his cooks never to serve them at Pemberley or Darcy House.

He heard Elizabeth suck in a breath beside him. Her eyes fairly danced with laughter.

Mr. Gardiner nodded enthusiastically, motioning for their party to follow him and addressing his son. "You heard the man yourself, James. If you wish to be as tall as Mr. Darcy, you will have to stop hiding them in your napkin." James' startled gaze darted up to his father.

Soaked and praying his boots would hold until they reached the carriage, Darcy could not help but chuckle. "Parents know everything."

Mr. Gardiner had not exaggerated when he said his carriage was nearby. Before the toe of Darcy's stockinged feet could peek between the sole and the leather of his unraveling boots, they stood by the conveyance.

He looked down at his sopping garments and inside at the clean, polished squabs.

Mrs. Gardiner handed Darcy the blanket draped over her arm. "This will ease your conscience."

He accepted the colorful covering and turned to Elizabeth. "My sister has several gowns from which you may choose a replacement. Please, Miss Elizabeth, allow me to make reparations."

Elizabeth reached inside the carriage and pulled out a redingote, which she donned over her damp dress. "Nobody is the wiser. I am only a little damp and shall make it back to Gracechurch Street on foot without any inconvenience. You, on the other hand…"

Bingley said, "I would be delighted to walk with the rest of our party to Darcy House. It is not far, and I could not wish for better company." He smiled at Miss Bennet, who blushed in response.

"May I accompany you, Papa? And Mr. Darcy?" asked James.

"I want to stay with the dog. What is her name?" asked Henry, feeding her another handful of crumbs from his pocket.

Richard took the boy to join his brother with the party of walkers upon hearing Mr. Gardiner say in a tone which brooked no argument, "I wish to have a word with Mr. Darcy."

The statement chilled Darcy to the bone. He knew what that meant. Although the prospect was not disagreeable to him, he could not imagine a worse circumstance to bring about his union with Elizabeth. Had one week seeing her sister happily restored to Mr. Bingley been enough to repair her opinion of him?

It was with sincere penitence and deep resignation that Darcy wrapped the blanket around his soaked breeches, told the driver where to direct them, and entered the carriage. Before the driver's whip snapped and the wheels jolted forward, Darcy said, "I apologize again for the scene in which your niece was caught, Mr. Gardiner. If it is reparation to her reputation you seek, please know that I am willing—"

"That is enough of that, young man. There is no need for a guilt-induced match when I saw the circumstances which led to what others might deem a compromise."

"But it was public. Her reputation—"

"Yes, that is unfortunate. However, as public as your embrace was, so were the circumstances which led to it. To insist on a match would only feed rumors that my niece choreographed the incident to catch a highly sought-after gentleman."

"Elizabeth would never—" Darcy bit his tongue, but it was too late. He had called her Elizabeth, an intimacy only allowed to a gentleman betrothed.

"I am pleased you know Lizzy well enough to believe her incapable of manipulative feminine arts." Though Mr. Gardiner's words were mild, he had not missed Darcy's blunder. His gaze was more intense than it had been. Leaning forward, he asked, "May I make a bold inquiry?"

Darcy did not feel himself in a position to refuse. Throat dry, he nodded his assent.

"Are you fond of my niece?"

"I am." Darcy's voice sounded gravelly and desperate in his own ears. Clearing his throat, he added, "Very much." He grimaced at the crack. What was he—a lovelorn juvenile?

Mr. Gardiner grinned. "Then I wish you all the advantages you shall need to win her heart."

Wealth, Darcy had. And position. An estate envied by the finest families in his circles.

The gentleman opposite him settled against the cushions. "Yes, you shall have to work doubly hard."

That ended Darcy's list-making. He had thought his advantages were impressive.

Her uncle spoke on, seemingly aware of Darcy's thoughts. "The very things which would draw most ladies shall prove to be obstacles to her. Lizzy is not impressed by common advantages. Wealth has no influence on her, and she is more apt to laugh at the haughtiness of the *ton* than seek their approval."

Darcy's heart plummeted as he recalled how often she had laughed at him, at her defiance when she refused to dance with him (when he had finally asked), at her unflagging boldness when his aunt had interrogated her about her family. The evidence was abundant and blatant. Why had Darcy not drawn the same conclusion before?

"For you to win her heart would be the greatest recommendation to your character any man could wish for. I am inclined to like you, Mr. Darcy, so I will warn you that you are not the only contender."

The carriage stopped, as did his heartbeat, which froze in his chest. Darcy saw his house through the window, but his head whirled. More contenders? Did he mean Wickham? Wickham had become adept at twisting his failures to his convenience; Elizabeth had been quick to defend the lout. Darcy could not hide his bitterness. "Miss Elizabeth is too perceptive for a false charmer to do much more than briefly turn her head. He cannot hold her interest."

"And are you confident you can?" Mr. Gardiner raised an eyebrow.

"Not at all." The admission hurt, but it was the truth. Without his wealth and status and all the comforts and advantages they represented, what *did* he have? Darcy preferred to think of himself as an honorable man, a responsible and attentive master, a devoted brother and cousin. But he had not made a good impression on Elizabeth or her neighbors.

Furthermore, he had done himself no favors by interfering with Miss Bennet's prospects. Had he been high-handed? He had been wrong. But had he been too assertive that his opinion was correct despite the proof in Bingley's heart?

Darcy could do better. He knew he could. Crushing his doubts with renewed determination, he added, "However, I intend to try."

Mr. Gardiner nodded solemnly. "Then I wish you well. You and I are men of action, accustomed to getting results. Me with my business and my family, and you have a reputation—do not be surprised, sir. My wife hails from Lambton, and she has nothing but praise for your estate, for the efficiency with which it is run, and which I, as a tradesman, recognize to be the work of a responsible, caring, and diligent master. Such qualities have a good chance of earning my niece's respect, if you allow her to see them."

Mr. Gardiner knew a great deal more than Darcy was comfortable with. Her uncle knew Elizabeth did not approve of him. Darcy's humiliation was complete. And yet the man sitting across from him was giving him hope

If only Darcy was not ruining Mr. Gardiner's squabs with every second he sat on the leather cushions. If only they had more time to talk. If only he was not indecently wet. "I will have refreshments sent to the parlor for you and the rest of our party."

"Thank you, Mr. Darcy, but Lizzy will wish to change into a clean gown, and the children will be tired."

Darcy bowed his head, heavy with defeat.

"However," Mr. Gardiner continued, "if you would be so gracious to accept an invitation to dine at my house along with Mr. Bingley and your cousin, I would be pleased to welcome your company."

"Thank you. I would be delighted." Darcy's reply was eager.

"You are not too fine to dine with a tradesman on the eastern side of Covent Garden?"

Darcy had to recognize that, before meeting Mr. Gardiner, he might have been hesitant. But the uncle's manners were those of a gentleman. The way he saw to his niece's comfort and those of a complete stranger recommended him more than many of Darcy's higher-born acquaintances. "I am honored to accept your invitation, and I am certain Bingley and the colonel shall be pleased to accept, providing they are not previously engaged."

"Of course." Mr. Gardiner tipped his head.

"I shall reply as soon as I am able so as not to inconvenience Mrs. Gardiner or your cook more than necessary."

Mr. Gardiner tapped on the door, and a footman opened it. "New friends are always welcome at our table, Mr. Darcy."

Darcy would like to be the Gardiners' friend.

Alighting stiffly from the carriage, he sloshed up the steps to Chalmers, who received him with pinched lips and furrowed brows but, fortunately, no questions.

CHAPTER 16

The dinner with Mr. Darcy, Colonel Fitzwilliam, and Mr. Bingley was so agreeable, the conversation so flowing and diverting, that Elizabeth could not but hope that the three gentlemen might call again the following day.

For a certainty, Mr. Bingley would. He called every day. But it was not Mr. Bingley Elizabeth most wished to see. (Nor was it the colonel, agreeable as he always was.)

James had snuck out of the nursery the previous evening to catch peeks of his tall hero from the corner, risking the chastisement of his nurse (who he now felt he was too big to need) and the kindly correction of his mother (who reminded him that boys who wished to grow as tall as Mr. Darcy must get sufficient sleep—a fact which the gentleman himself solemnly confirmed).

Aunt reminisced about her friends in Lambton, and

Mr. Darcy showed a surprising knowledge of the humbler families near his estate by informing her who had married and had children, who had moved away, and who remained. It was a side of him Elizabeth had not thought to see and of which she could not help but commend.

She was starting to learn much about Mr. Darcy that she approved. For instance, Mr. Bingley had engaged Uncle in a conversation over business matters, displaying a keen insight which delighted Uncle and would surely have brought on the disapproval of a highborn gentleman above such mundane matters. Instead, Mr. Darcy shocked Elizabeth by comparing estate management to owning a business, thus dignifying everyone at the table with ties (close or distant) to trade.

Her estimation of the gentleman was thrown thoroughly off-balance. Had this change not been in his favor, it would have troubled her quite a bit. She would not deny her family his agreeable company any more than she would deny herself the friendship of this kind, attentive version of Mr. Darcy.

However, she would take great pains not to display any pleasure at all on seeing him. She would be as unaffected by his presence as she was by Mr. Bingley's or the colonel's. She would not allow herself to be shaken from her opinions *too* easily!

And so, the following day, Elizabeth watched the front door, her patience waning as the minutes passed.

"Lizzy, if you do not stop fidgeting, you will have us all in a fit of nerves." Aunt glanced at her over the top of her embroidery. "Really, I am inclined to sympathize with your dear mother for enduring such flinches and twitches."

As though the universe conspired to prove her aunt's point, Elizabeth jumped at the loud tap of the knocker echoing up the steps to the drawing room. Jane glanced at the clock (as though she were not keenly aware of the hour) and blushed, confident in the identity of her caller. Elizabeth saw Aunt Gardiner's smile before she hid it behind her embroidery on the pretense of inspecting a stitch.

Pretending a renewed interest in her novel, Elizabeth shoved the book in front of her face and attempted to discern how many pairs of footsteps followed the butler up the steps.

The butler stood in the doorway and cleared his throat. "Mr. Darcy, Colonel Fitzwilliam, and Mr. Bingley, ma'am."

Biting her bottom lip to contain her smile, telling herself that the lightness she felt stemmed from her happiness for Jane, Elizabeth lowered her book as Mr. Darcy walked into the room. Her intention to appear unaffected was forgotten when his eyes locked with hers. The other gentlemen spoke, but she could not concentrate enough to make sense of their words.

"Where is Ruby?" she asked softly as he took a chair near her.

"Sound asleep after a long walk in the park."

She cracked a smile. That explained the whiff of bacon she thought she had smelled when he came to sit by her. "I hope the geese behaved."

He chuckled. "We gave them a wide berth."

"How is her training coming along?"

His chest puffed up just as her mother's did when speaking of Jane's beauty or Lydia's liveliness. "She has mastered several commands already—more than I had thought possible."

"Mr. Mansell would be delighted to know she has not given you too much trouble."

He leaned forward conspiratorially. Elizabeth was beginning to think that bacon ought to be a more common scent in gentlemen's cologne. "I would not quite say that. She has decided that both of us fit in my favorite chair, and I cannot sit to read without her slowly inching her way over to rest her head on my lap."

"Hardly troublesome!" she teased, enchanted with the tender image in her mind.

"I do not have the heart to read at my usual pace. She whines every time I lift my hand to turn a page."

Sometime during their little conversation, Aunt had sent for tea. After fifteen minutes of light chatter on a variety of topics from social engagements to the state of the roads between sips, she finally steered the conversation to the weather. "It is such a lovely day. It would be a pity to waste it indoors."

Mr. Bingley perked up even more in his seat. "If it is agreeable to you, perhaps we might enjoy a stroll around the block."

Colonel Fitzwilliam finished his tea, setting the cup gently on the table. "The Monument is nearby, is it not? I have not been since Darcy and I were boys racing each other to the top."

Aunt clasped her hands together. "What a delightful idea. The view is second to none, or so I have been told."

"You have not been to the top?" the colonel inquired.

"I will leave such adventures to you young people. After one has children, it becomes more appealing to have both feet on sturdy ground." While Aunt's smile softened the firmness in her tone, it left no room for any attempt at persuasion.

Aunt was decided, and with the enthusiasm of a mother intent on seeing to the pleasure of her charges, she ushered them out of doors and down the pavement toward the impressive structure marking the origin of the Great Fire of London.

Minutes later, they stood in front of the giant column of Portland stone where St. Margaret Church once stood. Elizabeth tilted her face back to see beyond the tip of her bonnet. The sun gleamed against the gilded urn of fire topping the column, making it appear as though it were aflame.

Mr. Darcy spoke from beside her. "Have you ever stood two hundred feet above the ground?"

She looked down before she lost her balance. "Hardly! The highest I have climbed is the thickest branch in the tallest apple tree in Longbourn's orchard."

He looked down at her. "Nobody will think less of you if you make it up part-way and discover a fear of heights." The corner of his lips lifted upward.

Elizabeth took his expression as a challenge. Arching her eyebrow, she asked, "Are you speaking from experience, Mr. Darcy?"

His laughter boomed, causing Mr. Bingley and the colonel, who walked ahead with Jane, to look back at him.

"Race you to the top, eh, Darce?" the colonel tossed over his shoulder.

"Do you have a penchant for defeat, Rich?"

Elizabeth bit her tongue to silence her mirth. This was hardly the stick-in-the-mud he had made himself out to be in Hertfordshire. Who knew that Mr. Darcy knew how to tease? The grin he bore, along with the daring gleam in his eye, was a welcome sight.

Colonel Fitzwilliam scoffed. "The stairs were slippery."

"I managed them well enough."

"Your boots were worn in, while I sported a newer pair. You can hardly fault me for not wishing to slip and tumble down that narrow, winding staircase."

"Excuses, excuses."

Elizabeth could contain her laughter no more. Dabbing the corners of her eyes, she calmed enough to ask, "Will we have the honor of witnessing a rematch today?"

Mr. Darcy turned his smile to her, and Elizabeth found it increasingly difficult to remember his faults. "I would rather enjoy the view than engage in sport." The way he said the words and the intensity with which he regarded her made her warm through. Did he mean the view from the top, or the view of her?

Colonel Fitzwilliam cleared his throat. "Then I will guarantee my victory and lead our jolly expedition up the stairwell."

Mr. Darcy held his arm out to Elizabeth. "Far be it for me to deny the old boy his victory." Together, they charged ahead of Mr. Bingley and Jane.

Three hundred eleven steps. Elizabeth tried to see the top from the bottom of the spiraling staircase, then thought better of it when the sight made her dizzy.

Mr. Darcy gestured for her to precede him. "The trick is to not look down."

"Or up," she said under her breath, planting her foot on the first stair and beginning the climb.

"Are you afraid?" he asked behind her.

She knew she should be, and yet she picked up her pace. She could not acknowledge a fear to Mr. Darcy or appear weak, no matter how reasonable her alarm might be. Any structure so tall that it blurred her vision and tipped her off balance should inspire a reasonable measure of fear. "While I greatly respect the laws of gravity, especially in moments such as this, I must also consider the solidity of the structure and the soundness of these steps."

"Very practical."

She noted with some satisfaction how clipped his words were between pants for breath.

Filling her lungs as full as her booming heart allowed, she added as airily as possible. "How thrilling to see London as the birds do. Above the spires. I wonder if we will be able to see The Globe. Or as far as Westminster?" She gasped for air. She dared not look up or down but guessed they must be at least half-way up the column.

"I will not spoil your surprise. You will see for yourself… soon enough. Did you know… this monument… is used as a… scientific instrument… to test various… gravity and pendulum experiments?… There is a laboratory… built underground." Mr. Darcy's breath was labored too, and Elizabeth could only guess that he continued their conversation to distract her from the disconcerting emptiness on the other side of the handrail.

If he was determined to converse, then she would do her best to reply with what precious little breath her lungs held. Her legs burned. She could only imagine how Jane fared below. Pointing to the top of the shaft, she asked, "Do scientists drop apples from there?"

"They should."

Elizabeth wondered what he and the colonel had dropped from the top.

"Every step… is precisely… six inches in height. … A constant environment… to conduct studies… on barometric pressure." Mr. Darcy sounded more like a guide on a tour than a companion enjoying an outing on a fine day.

"Shall we?" Deep breath. "Conduct an experiment, sir?" She turned to look at him, using their exchange to catch her breath.

"An experiment?"

"I hypothesize that with every six inches up this column, we shall find it more difficult to continue in conversation."

"We are part-way there."

Dear Lord, she had thought they must be part-way a while ago. She swallowed her disappointment. "That is a relief."

"You are not afraid?"

"No." Why did he insist?

"There is no shame in turning back. James Boswell —you are familiar with his works?"

"The Scottish writer." Elizabeth sucked in another breath and continued upward. "He wrote a biography of Samuel Johnson." Another pant. "They were friends."

"The very one. He suffered an attack of nerves right here. He considered the ascent horrid."

"I assure you, Mr. Darcy"—deep heaving breath— "I

am not in the least afraid." His insistence made her wonder if perhaps he was not entirely immune to their looming altitude. She paused, pivoting on her feet to face him. "Are *you* afraid?"

He stopped abruptly, only two steps below her, his eyes at the same level as hers. His pupils enveloped the golden-brown irises surrounding them, and he swallowed hard, his breath puffing against her hair and tickling her neck. "Not of heights."

Tilting her chin, she asked, "What *do* you fear, Mr. Darcy?" It was a bold question, and she did not expect a reply. She turned and resumed the trudge upward, her neck still tingling, her legs wobblier than they had been a moment before.

"Great Danes." He said the words so softly, Elizabeth thought she imagined them.

"Great Danes?" She paused, twirling around to see his expression. "But Ruby—"

He made a noise, something between a scoff and a gasp for air. "She is the rare exception."

"Yes, it was love at first stumble. I recall the evening well." She paused, allowing him the chance to fill in the details.

His jaw clenched, and he nodded at the square of blue sky through the opening at the top of the stairs. "We are close."

Interesting. Elizabeth felt her curiosity rise. Why *had* he called at the cottage that night? Had she liked him less, she might have pressed the matter. But she did like him—as she had finally admitted to herself—and she would not make him suffer to satisfy her curiosity.

Twirling around, she continued their progression up the eternal spiral.

An iron railing around the spare platform was the only security offered to the intrepid few who made it all the way to the base of the torch. At first Elizabeth hugged the column, but by the time she had circled to the other side looking over the square, she was brave enough to look over the edge.

Colonel Fitzwilliam stood at the railing, waving to the tiny people two hundred feet below them. "It is about time you joined me! I was worried you might have gotten lost."

Elizabeth joined him, and Mr. Darcy stood close to her other side, his hand so near hers on the railing, she doubted that even a slip of breeze could pass between them. She did not protest. In fact, his closeness comforted her. Should the railing give (unlikely, given its thickness), he would protect her from falling.

The realization that being the object of Mr. Darcy's protection did not provoke her usual rebellious ferocity to maintain her independence gave her pause. On what did she base this newfound trust? How could she be so certain he would not abuse her trust when that was precisely what most gentlemen did—especially those of his class, accustomed to getting their way?

She pondered the question while the colonel exchanged several jabs at Mr. Darcy's expense, to which he responded in equal humor. This both surprised and delighted Elizabeth, who was growing increasingly more willing to see Mr. Darcy's finer points now that she knew he was not the unapologetically high-handed, disdainful critic she had once believed him to be.

Bold enough to look over the edge, she saw Jane and Mr. Bingley waving at them from the street. She waved back. The height might have been too much for Jane. Or, perhaps it was Mr. Bingley who feared heights.

The colonel chuckled. "I would not put it past Bingley to proclaim a fear of heights so that he might have a few minutes of conversation with Miss Bennet."

"Would he take that kind of initiative?" Elizabeth asked, praying it was so. She had seen proof of Mr. Bingley's improved resoluteness, but she dearly wished for his reformation to be permanent.

"Any gentleman in pursuit of a lady's affection would go out of his way to make such opportunities," Mr. Darcy replied with a firmness that matched his strength of character.

Elizabeth had intended to ask the colonel of his opinion, but he must have continued around the platform, as he was now out of sight. Turning toward her remaining companion, she felt his gaze on her before she met his eyes with a bold look of her own.

Did he intend this as his own opportunity? If he did, for what reason? Elizabeth did not flatter herself. To allow herself to dream of an unequal match with such a man was a sure path to misery of the acutest kind. And yet, she could easily lose herself in the depths of his intense gaze. She could allow his attention to fuel her vanity and cause her to believe she truly was the one woman he would defy expectation and obligation to choose.

It was too tempting. Too dangerous. She admired him, but she could not claim to love him. Nor could she allow herself to cross that line. She had to lighten the tension between them.

"Why are you afraid of Great Danes?" she asked, turning the topic as far away from courtship and affection as she could summon in an eye blink.

CHAPTER 17

Darcy's heart plummeted two hundred feet. He had been so near to declaring himself. The pieces were in place—Bingley was wooing Miss Bennet at a convenient distance, Richard had wisely made himself scarce, and Elizabeth had not shied away at his bold speech. She could have no doubt about his affection. He had thought the timing perfect, but she had changed the subject in a blink.

He gripped the handrail, feeling off-balance. A man seeking to impress a woman did not wish to speak of his weaknesses. She would think him ridiculous, and he craved her respect. "It is only something I experienced as a boy. Hardly worth repeating."

She looked away, her smile dying. Blast. Now, he had disappointed her. He gritted his teeth, his knuckles white around the rail. He would rather suffer another hit to his pride than disappoint her.

Taking a deep breath, he said, "One of my father's tenants hailed from Kent. They had developed a certain attachment to the breed, and when they moved to Derbyshire, they brought a dog with them." That was the easy part to admit. Darcy took another deep breath, dreading the next part.

So intent was he on his own discomfort, Elizabeth's gentle touch on his arm released an unexpected shock of electricity through him. "Please, Mr. Darcy, if the story distresses you, I do not need to hear it. I trust you have your reasons, and that is enough." The softness in her expression, the tenderness in her eyes—for him! —turned his resolve on its head. Wild horses could not keep him from telling her his story now. If only she would continue to look at him as she did at this moment.

He gloried in her concern and continued before she thought to remove her hand from his arm. "You are kind to note my distress, but as Ruby has become a permanent part of my life, I had best address the source of my fright."

She moved her hand, and Darcy would have protested had he had any right to. "I had not thought you capable of fearing anything, Mr. Darcy."

While her words soothed his ruffled dignity, he would rather have her hand back on his arm. Feeling increasingly peevish as his longing progressed to desperation for her to put her hand back where it belonged, he said, "Above all things, I fear being unable to protect those who rely on me."

He wished his words unsaid the moment they crossed his lips. He had never voiced the fear that stole more of his slumber than any other, and while he would always be honest with Elizabeth, he had not intended to be *that* honest.

"A natural concern, and one I understand well. I would do anything to help my friends," she said, as though he had not bared his soul to her. He could have kissed her atop that intimidating tower for her understanding, with God as their witness… along with anyone who happened to look up at the fiery torch under which they stood.

Surely, she knew—how could she not?—that he wished to include her among those he was honored to protect. He would shield Elizabeth from her father's indolence, providing her with a secure place in Darcy's heart and a beautiful home in which to house it. He would use the strength of his name and reputation to safeguard her from any scandal her mother and younger sisters might cause. He had fortune enough for both of them and far too many connections for his taste. He was happy to share.

More than that, he would more willingly share this mortifying bit of history in the confidence that she would not only comprehend the futility of his fear; Lord knew, he understood its senselessness himself. If he was fortunate, she would sympathize with him.

Additionally, he had not yet given up on her comforting touch. Surrender was not in his nature. "Your friendship is not easily bestowed and therefore more worth the earning."

She sighed, her hand remaining determinedly on the railing. "Mr. Darcy, I hope you do not exclude yourself from my circle of friends, as small as it is."

He was her friend now. That was progress—most satisfactory progress. He was convinced that the happiest unions were those whose affection deepened over the years. He could think of nothing more exceptional than being his wife's dearest friend.

"Besides," she said, bumping him with her shoulder (quite purposefully, he thought), "if I wish to see more of Ruby, I had better make peace with and befriend her master."

Darcy laughed, now more at ease to share his story than he would ever be. "First, you must know my history with the breed to understand how extraordinary that puppy is for securing her place in my home. I was nine years of age when the incident happened." He felt her hand on his arm, and his heart felt so elated, it was a wonder he did not float into the clouds. Whether she realized what she did or not, he was unwilling to draw her attention to it lest she remove her hand from his arm once again. "I was with… a friend." He refused to mention Wickham. It would sour their conversation. "The son of a man my father respected highly and trusted."

She arched her brow, but if she suspected he referred to Wickham, she said nothing.

Darcy continued, "We were running over the fields, catching frogs and climbing trees, when we came upon the tenant's house. The dog laid in front of the door, and I saw how his ears perked up when we got near. I turned to continue down the field, but... my friend... began throwing rocks at the dog."

She gasped.

"The dog was as big as a Hereford cow. It charged after us, and I took off at a run."

She huffed. "I daresay your so-called 'friend' had already run out of harm's way or climbed up a tree, leaving you to face the angry guard defending his property."

He loved how quickly she rose to his defense. It was quite a shift from foe to friend, and Darcy savored the change. His suit was advancing nicely, he congratulated himself. "I did not see him again until I returned home with a hole torn in the back of my breeches." He still remembered the breeze on his backside as he tried to hide between trees and through shrubs all the way home; the brute had left little fabric with which to cover himself. Despite what Richard teased, there was no scar. Just an impressively sized bruise on his buttocks and an even larger one on his pride.

Elizabeth raised a hand to hide her smile, but there was no disguising her laughter. Darcy would have told the story all over again, for her other hand remained where it was on his arm.

~

RICHARD FAIRLY FLEW DOWN the steps. His plan had worked to perfection. If Darcy trusted Miss Elizabeth with a story Richard had teased and tormented his cousin with for years, then there was no doubt about the firmness of his affection.

Bursting out of the entrance, he ran over to Bingley and Miss Bennet. His grin widened as he drew nearer. First, he addressed the most urgent matter. Catching his breath and calming his excitement, he addressed Miss Bennet. "I can assure you with every fiber of my conviction that Darcy loves Miss Elizabeth in earnest."

"As you are convinced of it, I have no reason to doubt you, Colonel. However, is his love strong enough to survive the opposition certain to come his way once he makes his preference for my sister known? Lizzy is strong and not easily intimidated, but would not all of high society object to her—perhaps even a good part of his own family? I would hate to see her happiness dimmed with their attempts to make her feel inferior."

Richard rubbed his chin. "Aye, it is a proper concern." His gaze flickered over to Bingley, and he nodded at Miss Bennet. "If you do not do your best to deserve her, I know several gentlemen who would be delighted to take your place."

"I know it!" Bingley agreed, pink-faced. "You need not remind me of my good fortune. I feel I am the luckiest man in the world every moment I am in Miss Bennet's company."

There would be an engagement announced soon. Richard was glad for Bingley, but he would make certain to encourage his friend's decisiveness where he could. Help him along a bit. "You will have to explain why you did not join us. By now, I suspect that Darcy and Miss Elizabeth have discovered that I am no longer with them and are on their way down."

Bingley nodded. "I have that all sorted out. I shall admit to a severe aversion to heights."

Miss Bennet grinned. "I do not mind assuming the blame."

Shaking his head, Bingley stood firm. "I clutched onto you like a ninny and feel rather foolish for it. I have the entire story in my mind and can state it with conviction, knowing that it would have proven true not a quarter of the way up the stairs. I truly am afraid of heights." He swallowed hard and blushed so red he resembled a tomato.

She smiled at him fondly, and though she did not say *You dear man!*, her expression said it clearly enough.

Before any more plans could be schemed, Darcy and Miss Elizabeth joined them. Bingley performed brilliantly, as did Miss Bennet. Darcy had no idea the afternoon had not been a contrived plan executed down to every last detail.

Content with his success, Richard could hardly believe his further triumph when they returned the ladies to the Gardiners and Darcy astonished them all with an invitation to the theater.

CHAPTER 18

Aunt Gardiner and Jane's eyes shone as they discussed the marvels awaiting them at Harding, Howell & Co. Elizabeth wavered between curiosity and excitement. Mr. Darcy's invitation to the theater the following evening had offered the perfect opportunity for Aunt to indulge her nieces, something she always sought to do and did so generously. Elizabeth's skin tingled, and she smiled as she looked out of Uncle's carriage window, but her thoughts were far away from gloves and lace.

Mr. Darcy had shared a confidence with her—one which brought her no end of merriment at his expense. She could not look at a Great Dane without the rather humorous (and highly inappropriate) image of a young Master Darcy hiding behind bushes and trees, his bottom airing in the breeze for anyone to see. He had trusted her by exposing his mortification. As a result, her respect for him had deepened.

She so badly wanted for Mr. Darcy's behavior toward Mr. Wickham to be justified. It had been easy to side with Mr. Wickham, but that was before Mr. Darcy had proved himself capable of being likable, so approachable and easy to talk to, and funny. Was he capable of the deceit Mr. Wickham had described? Of denying a favorite of his own father the living bestowed upon him in his will? Elizabeth despised injustice—especially at the hand of the upper class toward one with few prospects. It was supremely unfair!

There had to be a reasonable explanation or perhaps, as Jane often said, a misunderstanding. If that were the case, then a mere question might prove to be the first step in establishing peace between the two gentlemen. Elizabeth would ask Mr. Darcy the following night. Only, how could she do so discreetly?

It struck her as significant that she had settled on Mr. Darcy to satisfy her inquiry. He would give her an accurate, truthful accounting. That was, if he deemed the matter worth speaking of. She could not force an explanation, though she hoped he might grant her one.

Mr. Wickham's conversation had entertained in the moment but, upon further consideration, left her unsatisfied. She did not want to cast him as deceitful, and yet how could she think of either gentleman with more esteem than the other without doing so?

Her aunt interrupted her thoughts. "Lizzy, I suggest you look away from the window if it only serves to provoke sighs. I have counted at least three in the last five minutes."

Turning away from the window, Elizabeth pasted a smile on her face that soon turned genuine when she saw her aunt's concern. "I apologize, Aunt. My thoughts took a ponderous turn."

Aunt squeezed her hand. "About Mr. Darcy?"

Elizabeth's cheeks burned. She wished she could lie, but Aunt would know it. So would Jane. Elizabeth's embarrassment would subside much quicker for admitting the truth than her own guilt at telling a falsehood would. "Yes."

"He is a handsome gentleman, and so attentive." Aunt patted her hand and leaned back to watch her with a narrow, calculating gaze.

It made Elizabeth nervous. "He is merely acting as a good friend should." She wondered if Mr. Darcy would call if he did not have Mr. Bingley to lead him to Gracechurch Street. Gentlemen of his status had no reason to tread that far east. They belonged to the fine mansions, swept pavements, and manicured gardens on the west side.

"Good friends make the best husbands." Aunt spoke the words softly, but their meaning hit Elizabeth like a thunderbolt.

She squelched the thought before it could take root. "I can assure you that Mr. Darcy could have absolutely no romantic interest in me. He is merely being kind."

Aunt bit her bottom lip and smiled. Jane pursed her lips and looked askance at Elizabeth.

"It is true!" Elizabeth insisted. "He told Mr. Bingley that I am not handsome enough to tempt him."

"People often improve in appearance on further acquaintance," Aunt commented.

Feeling her forehead tighten with a frown, Elizabeth voiced what she often repeated to herself. "He is merely righting a wrong, as any gentleman would do."

Aunt's eyebrows arched up in unison, two matching question marks. "Well, I for one am delighted that he has chosen to display his gentlemanly manner to you. I find his company pleasant, and your uncle enjoys his insights."

Crossing her arms, then realizing how churlish her posture must seem, Elizabeth folded her hands in her lap and tried not to scowl stubbornly or grin hopefully. Mr. Darcy provoked extremes in her, and while she was content to hate him before, she now feared for her heart.

Mr. Darcy was a gentleman. That was all. He accompanied Mr. Bingley to call on Jane just as often as Colonel Fitzwilliam did. There was nothing special about that. Was there?

She was still convincing herself of the platonic nature of Mr. Darcy's acquaintanceship—friendship?—when the coach stopped at 89 Pall Mall.

A crowd of ladies and their maids, gentlemen, and scattered footmen holding packages milled about, their every need and request attended by an employee of the shop. The haberdasher's at Meryton was half the size of one of the glass-partitioned departments inside Harding, Howell & Co.

Aunt led them through a menagerie of fur muffs, caps, and tippets lining the walls that waited for the colder months to come out in their soft, comforting glory. Painted fans spread over the counters and in displays, wielded by ladies who snapped them open with a flick of their wrists and batted their eyelashes over the edges while the clerk praised how well the color of the fans complemented the hue of each lady's eyes. This was just the sort of place in which Miss Bingley would like to be seen selecting the choicest silks to send to her exclusive French modiste.

They passed another glass partition, and Elizabeth stood in wonder at the overwhelming assortment of fabrics, lace, and gloves. Aunt marched confidently to the counter, securing a space between a gentleman and an overly provocative lady who had been attempting to capture his attention unsuccessfully, given the angle of the gentleman's back. Only when Elizabeth joined her and Jane did she recognize the gentleman valiantly ignoring the lady's suggestive advances.

"Mr. Wickham!" she exclaimed.

He dropped the rose petal pink kid gloves into the box on the counter and turned to her with a large-as-life smile. "Miss Elizabeth! Miss Bennet! How delighted I am to see you here!" His gaze swept past her to land on Aunt. "And I see you have another sister I have not yet had the pleasure of meeting."

Jane smiled. "Aunt Gardiner, this is Mr. Wickham. He has been stationed at Meryton with the regiment all winter."

He clutched his chest. "Aunt? I know you to be a lady of your word, Miss Bennet, but I never would have guessed this lady to be older than a cousin." He cast Elizabeth a look that made her laugh as he bowed elegantly. "Mrs. Gardiner, I am delighted to make your acquaintance. Your nieces have spoken so highly of your grace and wisdom, I did not imagine such a young woman could possess those qualities to the degree in which they were extolled."

Aunt returned his smile with a blush.

Elizabeth asked, "What brings you to London?"

He glanced at the pink gloves and looked around as he leaned closer to their cluster and spoke in a low tone. "A special commission from Colonel Forster. A gift for Mrs. Forster."

Jane clasped her hands by her face. "How thoughtful of him, and how kind of you to help when he is no doubt unable to see to the task himself."

Mr. Wickham tilted his head. "Anything to increase the happiness of my superior." There was a slight bitterness in his tone, but as neither Aunt nor Jane intimated they had heard it, Elizabeth supposed she might have imagined it.

His smile widening, he added, "There truly is more happiness giving than in receiving. Knowing I may contribute to someone's joy increases my own tenfold."

"Well said, Mr. Wickham," commented Aunt. "You must be a favorite in the village, as well as of your commanding officer for him to entrust you with the purchase of such a special gift for his wife."

A dimple flashed in his cheek, and his eyes danced merrily. "I merely attempt to reflect the charm and warmth with which I have been so graciously received. I have grown fond of the inhabitants of Meryton and its surrounding estates."

Aunt shot Elizabeth a meaningful look, which Elizabeth was grateful Mr. Wickham did not see, as he had caught the attention of the clerk behind the counter. "Wrap these up with a satin bow. Pink is the lady's preferred color."

No wonder Mrs. Forster and Lydia got on so well. Lydia would praise Mrs. Forster's superior taste (pink being her favorite color, too), and Lydia's flattery would be rewarded with the lending of little trinkets and fripperies.

Returning to them, Mr. Wickham bowed his head. "I regret I do not have more time to treat you ladies to ices or cake. The time of a lowly regimental officer is never his own to spend as he would most please." His gaze fell on Elizabeth.

"I am certain Mama shall invite you, Mr. Denny, and Mr. Chamberlain to Longbourn when we return from town next week." Elizabeth was certain he had enjoyed several meals there in her absence. If she could not secure any answers from Mr. Darcy, perhaps she might convince Mr. Wickham to reveal certain facts.

"I look forward to it, Miss Elizabeth." He deepened his bow and tucked the boxed gloves under his arm. "If you will excuse me."

He walked away, a fashionable figure in a sea of people.

Aunt leaned in until her shoulder touched Elizabeth's. "I can see why he is a favorite. Only be cautious, dear. He seems like a pleasant young man, but it is apparent that he is also expert in wielding his charm."

Something of which nobody would ever accuse Mr. Darcy! Elizabeth stood at the counter while her aunt and sister requested to see several pairs of gloves and multiple samples of lace. She nodded and pretended to pay attention, but once again, her thoughts were not on finery.

She enjoyed Mr. Wickham's company, his lively conversation, and charming manners… unlike Mr. Darcy, whose heavy thoughts darkened his eyes and oftentimes cast a brooding shadow over him. What troubled Mr. Darcy so much? Or was that simply his manner? Contemplative somberness with brief moments of sparkling, lighthearted laughter? Elizabeth doubted she would learn the answers to her many questions.

When she realized where her musings had once again led, she worried that she was becoming as meddlesome as her mother and Aunt Philips.

She shook her head. What was wrong with her? She hated to be wrong about people when she had always considered herself to be a great judge of character. But she had not been as happy to see Mr. Wickham as she would have been a few weeks ago. She nearly stamped her foot. Why did her opinion of Mr. Darcy matter? She cared no more for the gentleman than she did for Mr. Bingley or Colonel Fitzwilliam.

Except that was not entirely true.

CHAPTER 19

Darcy beat Bingley and Richard to the Gardiners' carriage. The footman flipped the step down, backing away but still within arm's reach to the entrance, eyeing Darcy suspiciously all the while. Darcy turned away from the disgruntled footman and held his hand out triumphantly, eager to display his gallantry. Unfortunately, he was rewarded—not with the delicate hand he had expected, but with thick, stubby fingers and hairy knuckles.

Mr. Gardiner guffawed. "I am sorry to disappoint you, young man, but I am not yet so old to be unable to see myself out of the carriage and assist the ladies."

Darcy was grateful for the breeze cooling his cheeks. He did not like feeling foolish. Forcing a smile, he stepped to the side, allowing Mr. Gardiner to alight and assist his wife to the pavement. Deciding that the best course was to make light of his blunder, Darcy stepped closer to the carriage and bowed with flourish.

When he stood, Bingley was beside him, practically shoving Darcy out of the way. He beamed brightly at his angel, and Darcy tried to maintain his composure at the sound of Richard's snickers behind him. Miss Bennet did not seem to notice; she had eyes only for Mr. Bingley. How Darcy had believed her indifferent, he no longer knew. It was apparent that she returned Bingley's devoted adoration in equal measure.

Elizabeth, on the other hand, had missed nothing. By the time her sister's foot cleared the step, she sat framed by the opening of the door, her eyes sparkling with glee and her laughter bubbling like water from a brook.

She wore the same dress she had worn to Bingley's Netherfield ball. However, she had done something clever with the lace trimmings which added an elegance and sophistication worthy of the theater. When she was Mrs. Darcy, he would ensure she never had to wear the same gown twice, though he doubted she would insist on filling her wardrobe with frothy frocks and flimsy slippers as most ladies did. No, his Elizabeth would be more impressed with a comfortable pair of half boots, the better with which to walk long distances. He smiled at the thought; he smiled at *her.*

Her touch was light, but the warmth of her hand seeped through their gloves, a promising portent of the evening ahead. Tonight was the perfect night. Bingley and Miss Bennet would be too enraptured with each other to pay him any heed, and Richard had already agreed to entertain the Gardiners so Darcy could sit beside Elizabeth.

He would take things slowly so as not to diminish her pleasure in the performance. Once he had seen to their group's refreshment during the intermission, he would ask the question burning in his heart and keeping him awake at night. He would ask her to be his wife, whereupon he would immediately seek Mr. Gardiner's approval. Mr. Bennet's would have to wait until the morrow.

They followed their party the short distance to the immense columns at the entrance of the theater. Elizabeth leaned into his arm, tugging until he leaned toward her and making him delirious with happiness at her nearness. "If I may presume on your confidence during the course of the evening, there is a matter—a question—I dearly wish to ask you." She tilted her chin up, the uncertainty in her eyes filling him with a protective urge to reassure her, and the desire to taste her lips.

But they were at Covent Garden, and a kiss in public here would be ruinous. He could not treat her like anything less than the lady he would honor for the rest of his life.

She had a question, too. He prayed it was not the same. He had heard a few cases of an impatient lady proposing matrimony to her dawdling suitor, but he had never thought to find himself in that situation. Coming from Elizabeth, a lady who knew her own mind, he should be flattered. Standing erect, he focused on her words. She had something important to ask him —nothing more, nothing less. "A happy coincidence, for there is a matter I also wish to discuss with you."

He squeezed his eyes shut for an instant, wishing for an eloquence his nerves simply would not allow. Why would he ruin her surprise by hinting at it now? Furthermore, how could he imply his matter was mundane when the question he burned to ask her was life-altering? Dear Lord, how was he supposed to endure until the intermission? That was hours away!

Further discussion was prevented when they caught up with their party, and Darcy led the way up the red-carpeted stairs to his family's private box. By the time they reached the balcony overlooking the stage and had settled to everyone's satisfaction, he determined that no matter how he burst to propose that night, he would allow Elizabeth to speak first. It was the gentlemanly thing to do.

The curtain opened, and the show began. He had thought the first half of the performance would lag at an unendurable pace, but watching Elizabeth made the time pass pleasantly. She laughed and clapped and stared with fixed interest and open mouth at every scene, sharing her rapture with him with frequent glances.

Twice she forgot herself enough to tap his sleeve

and exclaim without looking away from the scene to ensure he did not miss what so delighted her. Her awareness of him despite her captivating fascination for the theater warmed Darcy from head to toe, turning his limbs to putty. Her joy and enthusiasm encouraged him to dream. He imagined introducing his beloved betrothed to Georgiana. Elizabeth's charm, her humor and jubilant spirit would be the perfect antidote to his sister's recent melancholy. She had been for his.

Colors were brighter and the wonder Darcy had believed forever lost since his mother's death had returned in all its vivid splendor. Elizabeth had done that. And after tonight, she would be his betrothed.

When the curtain dropped, announcing the beginning of the intermission, Darcy jumped up so quickly that his chair toppled and he had to spin around to catch it before it tipped over.

Richard smirked. Elizabeth looked concerned. "You are leaving so soon?"

For a moment, Darcy's breath caught in his throat. She did not want him to go. Had she imagined them sitting by the fire at Pemberley as he had, comfortable in silence, content in each other's company?

She added in a whisper, "The question."

He understood. He felt the same. But their refreshment would not make its way to them on its own. The sooner he brought them lemonade, the sooner he could resume his place beside Elizabeth. The sooner she could ask her important question, and the sooner he could ask his. "I shall not tarry." Turning to his friend, he called, "Bingley."

Elizabeth hid a smile behind her gloved hand when Bingley showed no indication he was at all aware of his surroundings beyond Miss Bennet.

"Bingley," Darcy said louder.

No response. Nudging his friend's foot with his boot, Darcy repeated, "Bingley!"

Bingley startled to attention, Miss Bennet reaching out to stabilize his chair. "Ah, yes?" He looked around him, understanding slowly replacing his befuddlement. Raising a finger in the air, "Refreshments! I shall accompany you to fetch refreshments."

Richard rose. "I would accompany you, but I think I spotted my mother with her sister and Lady Anglesey. If I do not make an appearance, I will not hear the end of it." He stood. "If I am correct, I shall be honored to make introductions. However, I think it prudent to first ascertain her identity before dragging you across the theater in this crush."

Elizabeth smiled without the least amount of trepidation at the possibility of being presented to two countesses. "That is very considerate of you, Colonel. I am dying to ask Jane's opinion of the first two acts." The Gardiners nodded in agreement.

Richard bowed, promising a prompt return. The curtain to the box had not closed fully behind Darcy when he heard Elizabeth whisper, "Did he ask?" Darcy turned to Bingley, horrified that his friend might have chosen the same night to propose as he had. Would his happiness be doubled or halved in the sharing of it? Looking at Bingley bouncing at his side, Darcy blurted, "Did you ask her?"

"Tonight? Surrounded by so many people? I would love to, but Jane is much too modest to wish to be the center of attention. She would feel pressured to consent, and I would feel like a heel."

Darcy had not considered that. Would Elizabeth feel likewise? She was not shy, but neither did he wish to coerce a favorable reply. Then again, she had flatly refused to dance with him at Sir William's dinner party, and there had been a few observers then. Would she refuse him now? His palms sweat at the possibility.

But she had an important question too. Surely he understood her better now than he had last winter. He had been a pompous fool then. Surely he had improved in her measure over the past few weeks, just as she had grown in his esteem. Surely!

Bingley's expression turned serious. "You look positively ill, Darcy. Are things not going according to plan?"

Darcy grumbled, "What do you know about my plan?"

Bingley's gaze darted around the lobby. "Oh, nothing. I just supposed that you had a plan; you always do." The longer he avoided meeting Darcy's eyes, the stronger grew Darcy's suspicion that Bingley knew more about his plan than he wished to reveal.

With a grimace, Darcy turned to the table to request seven lemonades. He wound his fingers around the stems of four of the glasses while Bingley balanced the other three.

It had been a perfect evening thus far, and Darcy was determined not to allow anything to ruin it. Elizabeth was enjoying herself. Would she not appreciate how romantic their setting was—how well it lent itself to a proposal? Perhaps during the final song when the hero professed his undying devotion to the heroine? Yes, that would be perfect. He would offer Elizabeth her own happy ending to the evening; a beginning to what Darcy hoped would be their eternal happiness together.

His enthusiasm renewed, Darcy clipped a gentleman brushing past on the shoulder. "My apologies," he uttered.

CHAPTER 20

"Darcy!" said the gentleman Darcy now recognized as Lady Anglesey's son. His name, Viscount Ponsonby, had been splashed all over the papers for the past week when he announced his engagement to Lady D'Abernon. "Mother said she thought she saw you sitting next to a charming creature. If you aim to beat me to the altar, you had better make haste!"

Darcy bowed, granting his jovial companion the deference his title merited. Bingley waited a few paces up the hall. "So I had heard, My Lord. Allow me to offer my congratulations." He nodded toward Bingley, ready to perform introductions.

Lord Ponsonby ignored him. Angling closer to Darcy to Bingley's exclusion, he said, "Emily is a lady any gentleman would be proud to have on his arm. I am fortunate."

Her thirty thousand pounds likely had something to do with that. It was no secret that Ponsonby had expensive taste, and his mother had seen fit to secure an heiress for her eldest son. Darcy hoped the wife would have more success instilling better manners in the gentleman than his mother had.

Bingley quietly slipped away, waiting a few paces at the edge of the hallway. He was too good-natured to fret over Ponsonby's snub, but Darcy could not forgive so easily. Determined to cut their conversation short, Darcy bowed and made to leave.

Ponsonby elbowed Darcy in the ribs and leaned in as though they were old chums. "Who is this extraordinary young lady who has caught your eye? Mother will want to know."

Always doing his mother's bidding! Darcy should have known he would not get away from Ponsonby until he had extracted enough gossip from him to satisfy Lady Anglesey.

Before the curtain dropped that evening, all the elite inside the theater would know the name Bennet. Elizabeth would be the subject of talk in every drawing room in London on the morrow. Let them talk. He was not ashamed of her, and Darcy would dare even Lady Anglesey to find any fault in Elizabeth. Proudly, Darcy replied, "Miss Elizabeth Bennet of Longbourn in Hertfordshire."

Ponsonby scratched his chin, his brows furrowing. "I do not believe I have heard the name."

Darcy sucked in a breath, forcing a pleasant manner. "I am hardly surprised. They are not often in town." Knowing how society frowned on such an admission, Darcy added with a smile, "Some of us prefer a quiet life in the country."

"Hertfordshire, you said? I am often a guest at Hatfield House, and I do not recall meeting the Bennets." He was like a dog with a bone he would not relinquish.

"Why should they depart from their perfectly comfortable estate?" Let Ponsonby make of that what he would. Again, Darcy attempted to redirect the conversation. "If I could, I would never leave Pemberley."

"Is the older gentleman with you her father?"

Darcy hissed through his forced smile. This was getting tiresome. "That is her uncle, Mr. Gardiner." He did not mention the address of his residence, and he most certainly would not offer that he was in trade.

Holding up the glasses balanced in his hands, Darcy said, "I must not keep the ladies waiting. If you will excuse me. My regards to Her Ladyship." With a bow, Darcy stepped into the current of gentlemen making their way back to their seats before the viscount could ask additional questions.

Bingley stepped in beside him, jutting his head over his shoulder and saying excitedly, "Is that not Mr. Wickham from the militia? I wonder what he is doing in town."

Some of the lemonade spilled over Darcy's gloves in his haste to glance behind him. His mouth went dry, his tongue thick. Why was Wickham here?

Darcy's box was only a few paces away. The curtain's fringe still fluttered. A cold chill crept down Darcy's back. First Pompous Ponsonby and now the Wastrel Wickham.

Bingley entered the box. "You will never guess who we passed in the hall." He did not know half of Wickham's sins, only that he was a mutual acquaintance.

"Mr. Wickham?" Elizabeth guessed, her eyes piercing Darcy. Her cheeks were flushed and her eyes bright, just as she had looked the day she had walked to Netherfield Park to care for her sister. He looked away, feeling sick. Did she favor Wickham? He had a way of making himself a favorite, but surely she had seen through his ruse by now!

Handing off the lemonade before he spilled any more, Darcy returned to his spot beside Elizabeth. Their fingers brushed when she took her glass, but where previously his yearning had filled him with sunshine and butterflies, it now filled him with pain.

What was Wickham about? Darcy had struck fear in him at their last meeting, and the ingrate had possessed sense enough to avoid him at Meryton. He had bowed out of attending Bingley's blasted ball. What had changed?

Elizabeth's skirts rustled as she turned to face him; her spicy citrus perfume whirled around him, drawing him in. He could not resist it. "You said there was something you wished to discuss with me?" she asked.

Darcy's gaze scanned over the crowded pit, and there he was. Wickham pretended to tip his hat. Even in the poorly lit pit, Darcy saw his smirk.

Taking a deep breath to compose himself, Darcy spoke through his tense jaw. He could not propose now. "Another time. It is nothing which cannot wait." Blast Wickham! Blast him for casting his poisonous shadow over the evening. Darcy could not propose with that man looking below. He smiled weakly at Elizabeth, not wanting her to feel his vexation or believe herself the cause of it.

"Oh." Elizabeth looked down at her hands, folding them together in her lap. "Well, then, I shall wait." The forced cheer in her tone nearly undid Darcy. His anger yielded to frustration—how many times must a man summon the courage to propose only to have his efforts disrupted at every turn?

Changing the subject, he asked, "You said there was something you wished to ask me?" He did his level best to appear congenial.

She sighed and took a sip of her drink. "It is nothing. A trifling matter best kept for another time."

They slowly drank their lemonade and tried to smile when Richard described the obstacles he had encountered crossing the crowded theater, only to learn that the lady sitting with Lady Anglesey was none other than Lady D'Abernon. They unanimously agreed that Lady Matlock would be flattered at her son's mistake and therefore should be told of it. Darcy smiled and nodded, but Richard noticed his ill-humor.

Darcy and Elizabeth watched the rest of the play in silence, his discomfort magnified by the animated conversation surrounding them. Elizabeth did not tap his arm, nor did she smile as much as she had before the intermission.

Across the theater, he saw Ponsonby whispering in his mother's ear. Lady D'Abernon listened in, hiding her reactions behind a well-placed fan. They looked shocked and displeased—a dangerous mix when it came to malicious, disparaging gossip.

The lovers on the stage reunited, the final curtain dropped, and Darcy's unasked question tasted like ashes on his tongue.

RICHARD PULLED Bingley aside as the ladies retrieved their wraps. "What happened?"

Bingley shook his head. "I hardly know! We fetched the lemonade, and Viscount Ponsonby waylaid Darcy, asking all sorts of questions about Miss Elizabeth and her family."

Richard groaned. He should have known his attempts to distract his mother's dearest friend would be in vain. Lady Anglesey had eyes like a falcon, and the fact she had not attempted to extract any information out of Richard while she had the chance could only mean she was already scheming.

"I thought Darcy handled himself rather well. Even tried to lighten the conversation." Bingley shrugged.

"That is promising, but all my mother's friends will be abuzz on the morrow, and I fear Darcy's reaction may not be to Miss Elizabeth's advantage." He rubbed his jaw, pondering how best to proceed.

"And then Mr. Wickham made an appearance," Bingley added. "I know Darcy does not like the gentleman, and now the Bennets and the Gardiners are certain of his aversion, too."

"Yes, I noticed. It is unfortunate. Wickham appears the long-suffering, charming victim, and Darcy looks the boorish curmudgeon."

Wickham was the least of Richard's worries, though. The lout would get overconfident, as he always did. Why else would he dare draw near either Richard or Darcy after what he attempted at Ramsgate? He believed that a life of privilege was his due, and his petty revenges against those who opposed him—mainly Darcy—would be to Wickham's detriment. Give Wickham enough time, enough rope, and he would hang himself.

No, the real enemy—the foe which could cause the most damage—would come from Darcy's peers. From his own family. And Darcy's response would mean the difference between a lifetime of felicity with the lady of his heart or a lifetime of regret.

CHAPTER 21

Darcy's disconcerting thoughts deepened during the night, and he could not bring himself to accompany Bingley to Gracechurch Street the following morning. Or the next.

Grabbing Ruby's leash, he set out across town, his thoughts thick and his steps heavy.

If Elizabeth preferred Wickham over him, then she was not the woman he thought her to be. It was easy to cast the blame elsewhere—to curse Wickham for his deception, to condemn Elizabeth for her prejudice.

But such accusations did not last long before Darcy dismissed them (albeit reluctantly). Darcy would shoulder the blame as he always did. If Elizabeth had a false impression of Wickham, it was because Darcy had made such an unchivalrous impression on her that she was willing to believe Wickham's lies. That was the crux of the matter. And Darcy despised himself for it. Of what use was his pride if it meant losing Elizabeth? To Wickham!

The theater loomed ahead of him and, once again, his frustration at having another proposal interrupted turned to relief. Elizabeth might have refused. He might have gained some ground, but she could not respect him if she believed Wickham's lies. And Darcy would not be content with only half of her heart when his love for her was complete.

He must try harder—cautiously, intelligently. Wickham could have his small victory, but in the end Darcy would prove himself to Elizabeth. Then, and only then, would Darcy have peace.

Unless she did not want him. His stomach twisted and churned at the possibility.

Reaching down to pat Ruby, who had not once crossed in front of his feet or pulled against her leash, he also removed a piece of bacon from his pocket. Raising it so she could see and smell her prize, he signed for her to sit. Her tail never stopped wagging, but she sat, her front paws prancing impatiently for her reward.

Darcy fed her the bacon. He did not have to reach as far down as he had only three weeks ago. "Good girl, Ruby." Two thumbs up. She looked up at him adoringly.

"Shall we return home, or continue on?" He pointed

as he spoke, and she followed the movement of his hands before a nearby fishmonger and the many odors from his cart could prove too tempting for her to ignore. Taking her interest as encouragement to continue, Darcy and Ruby walked past Lincoln's Inn, then St. Paul's Cathedral.

If he had told Elizabeth about his history with Wickham, would it have made a difference? He continued down Cannon Street, lamenting his lost opportunity for half of a block. If he told her his side of the story now, which was certain to contradict Wickham's embellished, vilifying tale, Darcy would appear vindictive. That was not an option.

He arrived at the place he did not, until then, realize he had been directing his steps. The Monument.

"Mr. Darcy!" a voice he would always heed called out to him.

He turned to see Elizabeth and Miss Bennet by the engravings at the base of the stone column. He sucked in a breath and reached down to touch Ruby, making certain he was not dreaming when his deepest desire had manifested the lady he most wished to see.

The dog licked his fingers. Elizabeth was real. And now that Ruby had seen her friend, she tugged against her leash for the first time that morning, pulling Darcy closer.

ELIZABETH HAD NOT MEANT to say Mr. Darcy's name so loudly, but her surprise was too great. Mr. Bingley called every day, but Mr. Darcy had not accompanied him since the theater. She had no idea if the gentleman meant to accompany Mr. Bingley on his return to Netherfield Park. She hoped so.

Jane pretended an intense interest in the landmark's carvings, leaving Elizabeth alone with Mr. Darcy and Ruby, who was determined to pull her reluctant master closer. He looked miserable. He looked everywhere but at Elizabeth, while she saw no one but him.

When Mr. Darcy perfunctorily scolded Ruby, "There shall be no bacon for you, young miss," Elizabeth's apprehensions melted away at the antics of their furry friend.

"I do not have any bacon, but I can scratch the spot you like under your chin," she offered, extending her hands for a happy puppy eager to snuggle. "Ruby has grown!" Elizabeth peeked at Mr. Darcy. He looked so uncertain of himself, passing Ruby's leash from one hand to the other, head down, and smelling deliciously of bacon, Elizabeth's boldness doubled to make up for his lack.

"Have you been well, Mr. Darcy?"

"Yes, thank you," he replied in a tone which belied his words. "And you? I hope you and your family are well?" He struggled to get the words out.

Elizabeth widened her smile to ease his discomfort.

Despite their tense silence at the theater, she was pleased to see him. "We are. Uncle is conveying Jane and me to Longbourn soon, and we decided to take a short walk before we must depart."

"You like to walk," he stated.

She was flattered he knew that about her. And that he cared enough to remember. "Yes, I do." She looked around him for one of Mr. Darcy's conveyances and saw none waiting. "It appears that you do too."

He cracked a smile. That was better.

Emboldened to ask the question foremost in her mind, she gave Ruby one last pat and stood to face Mr. Darcy. "Do you mean to return to Hertfordshire with Mr. Bingley?" She held her breath and hoped.

"Bingley keeps inviting me."

"And do you mean to accept his invitation?"

He hesitated, his gaze intensifying as though he were attempting to read her thoughts. "Would it please you for me to accept?"

"Of course." The reply slipped from her lips, sincere and eager. She did not want this to be the last time she saw Mr. Darcy.

She had yet to ask him about Mr. Wickham, and it occurred to her that unless she seized the opportunity, she might not have the chance to ask him again. Before she could convince herself not to indulge her inquisitiveness, she asked, "What happened between you and Mr. Wickham?"

His answer was not immediate. Far from looking

disappointed or disgusted, he seemed to be collecting his thoughts. When he finally spoke, his voice was deep and steady.

"I know you to be an intelligent lady, fully capable of discerning a man's true character without my interference."

A man's true character? Did that mean she was mistaken in her view of Mr. Wickham? "Are you saying he is not entirely honorable?"

"What I am saying is that I trust you to accurately discern his character. And to act accordingly."

He expressed a great deal more confidence in her than Elizabeth felt for herself. She could not help but recall how thoroughly she had misunderstood Mr. Darcy's essence. How badly had she mistaken Mr. Wickham's?

His eyes softened, as did his tone. "A gentleman proves himself by his actions, not his words."

Elizabeth could not argue with him about that. How they applied to the gentleman standing before her, though, was revealing. He had said some unfortunate things against her vanity, against Jane, against their family. But his recent actions had in every way proven him to be a gentleman. She had forgiven him.

"Mr. Darcy—" She did not know what to say or how to say it, but she felt that something had changed between them. Covering her lack of words with a weak smile, she said, "Thank you for trusting me."

That was it. He trusted her. She felt the depth of his

esteem. It humbled her to her bones. She would not give him cause to regret, she decided.

With a bow and a look that burned an impression on Elizabeth's heart, Mr. Darcy turned and left.

CHAPTER 22

Shoulders stiff, hands clasped behind his back, Richard paced the length of Bingley's study. Bingley sat at his desk, staring unseeingly at the untouched box of macarons under his nose. Richard spun around to face him, his voice sharp. "You have definitely invited him?"

"So many times, any more would be offensive." Bingley slumped in his chair.

Darcy was not the sort to be manipulated, and he would resent their attempt if they overplayed their hand. Richard resumed pacing. There simply had to be a way to unite them. His cousin was a good man—the best—but Richard had seen Miss Elizabeth's effect on Darcy. She brought out the best in him. She was the cream to Darcy's coffee; the spice in his stew.

Darcy could manage an estate profitably and provide for hundreds with a dignity and respect that won over their loyalty, but he clearly had no clue how to properly woo a lady and secure his own happiness. Richard cared for his inept cousin too much to allow him to bungle his opportunity with a lady so perfectly suited to him. If only that blasted Ponsonby and infernal Wickham had not shown up to ruin everything.

"What happened? What else did you observe?"

Bingley shrugged. "All I remember is that Darcy seemed to be floating on clouds on the way to the refreshment table. The viscount chilled him some, but seeing Wickham was what brought on the thunderclouds."

Wickham was a distraction from the real problem, but how could he get Darcy to see beyond the pesky fly to address the source of the rot?

"What did Miss Bennet say about Wickham?" Richard asked.

"She only commented that it was pleasant to see an acquaintance at the theater and that her mother and sisters would be sad about his absence from Meryton."

Richard frowned and rubbed his fingers over his chin. "Yes, he has a way with females."

"If only Darcy possessed a fraction of his charm," Bingley lamented, absently plucking a macaron from the box and taking a bite.

"Wickham's charm is superficial. He makes friends easily, but he has no talent for keeping them."

Bingley swallowed. "You do not have to tell me that.

I do not know everything that has transpired between him and Darcy—nor do I wish to know—but Wickham has developed a reputation in certain circles. He will soon run out of easy opportunities to pluck."

Wickham would eventually ruin himself. Without Darcy's support, it was a race to the dregs of society. He had been warned, but Wickham was too lazy and self-indulgent to lift a finger for his own betterment. In the meantime, he was a thorn in the side—a pest of the first order.

Richard ran his hand over his face. "The Bennet sisters return to Meryton today?"

Bingley nodded. "Mr. Gardiner has business with Mr. Philips and is conveying the ladies to Longbourn."

"When will you leave for Netherfield?"

"Next Monday. Sooner if I am able to wrap up the arrangements." The certainty in Bingley's tone was an agreeable sound. Now that Miss Bingley was discharged from Bingley's household to Mrs. Hurst's, his confidence had grown, and with it, so had his decisiveness.

Resuming his pacing, Richard marched with his hands clasped behind his back. "We have one week to convince Darcy to join you."

"My efforts have not proved successful. Do you have another strategy in mind?"

Richard did, but Darcy was announced along with Miss Ruby before he could explain it.

Bingley jumped up from his desk, making kissing

noises and waving his hands in welcome to his tongue-lolling guest. He opened up his hands, and Darcy dropped Ruby's leash so she could go to him. Then he lifted his palm to his shoulder, and she sat on his foot. Bingley was delighted.

"I think she likes you and means to keep you." Richard chuckled. "How is my favorite boot-licker?" he cooed.

Stretching over to the desk without moving his foot, Bingley nudged the box of macarons closer. "Can she have one, Darcy?"

Darcy pulled a piece of bacon out of his pocket and handed it to Bingley.

"That is where that smell comes from! You will have high society requesting 'a rich, but subtle blend, with top notes of bacon' from the perfumers."

Pulling his attention back to the more immediate matter, Richard caught Bingley's eye and winked. He would need him to play along if his plan would succeed. Clearing his throat, Richard said casually, "I have decided to accept Bingley's invitation to Netherfield Park. I simply must see this fine estate of which I have heard so much praise and decide for myself if he has exaggerated the beauty of the local ladies. I hope you mean to come too, or it would be awkward."

Darcy looked at him askance. "How is that? You can be Bingley's guest just as well as I can."

Before Richard could press further, Bingley exclaimed, "I would rather both of you be my guests!

You know how I abhor an empty house." He shivered and pushed the box of macarons toward Darcy. It was a good sign that Darcy was agreeable enough to accept. First step, macaron. Step two, Netherfield.

Leaning over the box of assorted flavors, Darcy asked, "What are you planning to do without a hostess? I take it your sisters are not invited?"

"Lord, no!" Bingley flinched, and Ruby decided it was high time to explore the room. Nose to carpet, she sniffed, looking up to Darcy every so often and returning to her explorations after he nodded at her, his eyes brimming with unbridled affection. Richard shook his head. If only Darcy could behave with Miss Elizabeth as he did with that dog, the lady would be certain to fall in love with him.

"In fact, since you are both here, I shall tell you that I aim to give Netherfield a proper mistress soon when I propose to Jane." Bingley blushed and sat on top of his desk, quickly adding, "I am not asking for permission or opinions, mind you. I merely wish to inform you of my decision. I will not be swayed."

Darcy swallowed his morsel. "Nobody would attempt it when congratulations are in order."

Richard scowled at Bingley. How would they get Darcy to join them at Netherfield Park after that announcement? He would worry they would hamper Bingley's courtship and in the way of the new mistress. Rubbing his chin again, Richard did his best to direct the conversation back to his target. "I suppose the three of us can muddle along until that blessed event." He watched Darcy for a reaction but got nothing. Blast his cousin's inscrutable countenance.

"You forget, Jane has yet to agree. After what I put her through, I half expect her to refuse my offer."

"You are willing to expose yourself to rejection?" Darcy asked, sitting in front of the desk and reaching for another macaron. Richard supposed Darcy had never considered the possibility of being rejected until Miss Elizabeth. Richard was glad Ruby had saved him from such a defeat when there were kinder ways for a man to be humbled—such as being attacked by geese.

Bingley replied, "I love Jane, but I know I do not deserve her. If she allows me to prove the steadfastness of my heart and agrees to become my wife, I will do everything in my power to make her happy and to be the man she desires. If she refuses me, then I shall wait and work and hope until I either win her trust... or she marries another."

Richard dabbed the corners of his eyes. "That is touching, Bingley. I wish you well."

Darcy returned to more practical matters. "In the meantime, you have an excellent housekeeper in Mrs. Nicholls."

Bingley smiled. "She will be elated that Caroline will not be there making unreasonable demands."

Bingley and Darcy ate the last of the macarons, and Richard pondered how best to proceed. He could not appear to be trying too hard; Darcy would see through him.

With a sigh, Richard crossed the room to the door. "If I am to convince my mother to leave me out of her plans for the season after this week, I had best begin my placations without delay."

Darcy rose, summoning Ruby with the spread of his arms. "We shall accompany you."

"To Matlock House?" Richard watched Darcy. "Or to Netherfield?"

Darcy glared at him but said nothing. He did not refuse either. That was progress!

Looking beyond Darcy, Richard saw Bingley grin and raise his thumbs. Richard walked a little lighter. They would have Darcy in Hertfordshire within the week.

CHAPTER 23

Uncle Gardiner left his carriage at Longbourn, deciding to continue the short distance to Mr. Philips' Meryton office afoot.

He and his two nieces stepped inside Longbourn, and the scene awaiting them was exactly as Elizabeth had expected: Papa was in his book room. Mary sat at the pianoforte. Mama occupied the settee with a view of the road, a bottle of smelling salts nearby. Kitty and Lydia were not in, being more interested in the officers who frequented their aunt's house than in receiving their eldest sisters.

Thus, after a quick refreshment and repast, Elizabeth decided to walk into Meryton with her uncle, her mother (who would have preferred to take the carriage but was significantly outnumbered), and Mary.

Mrs. Forster arrived at Aunt Philips' home shortly

after Uncle Gardiner deposited them at the front gate and promptly joined Kitty and Lydia on the settee while Aunt served everyone tea and cake. Mama and Aunt were much more interested in Jane's reunion with Mr. Bingley than in Elizabeth's stay with Charlotte and Mr. Collins, so after a respectable time, Elizabeth went to Mary, who sat alone by the window. "Would you like to accompany me to the circulating library?"

Mary looked about the room, at the clusters from which she preferred to distance herself, and nodded. "Thank you, Lizzy. Maybe they will have some new edifying pamphlets."

"One can only hope." Elizabeth struggled to keep her face straight as they walked past the gate to the cobblestone street.

"Do not pretend you enjoy them when I know very well you do not."

Slipping her arm through Mary's, Elizabeth owned, "You are not as easily deceived as I have been, Mary."

"Nonsense. Everybody knows you surpass me in every accomplishment." Had Mary sounded bitter, Elizabeth would have let the comment go by uncontested. But the impassive acceptance in Mary's tone stirred Elizabeth.

Stopping, she looked Mary in the eye. "I wish you would not say that, for it is not true." She saw Mary's disbelief as plain as the brown in her sister's eyes.

It became imperative for Elizabeth to prove her point, to give Mary something entirely of her own of which to be proud. Elizabeth felt shame for not having done so for her sister years ago. She would talk to their father and insist he hire a music master. If Lydia and Kitty could waste their pin money (and any extra they could convince him to part with) on bonnets they never wore and ribbons they discarded after one use, then the estate could afford a tutor for Mary.

Colonel Forster stepped outside of the haberdasher's just then, and Elizabeth sensed another opportunity. Tugging Mary down the street, she greeted the gentleman. "Colonel Forster, how pleasant to see you after so recently exchanging pleasantries with Mrs. Forster at our aunt's."

"So that is where she was off to! I had suspected as much."

It seemed strange to Elizabeth that a newly married man responsible for a regiment did not know where his young wife was, nor whose company she kept. But Elizabeth had another question to settle, and she would not allow her musings to distract her from her purpose. "My sister Jane and I recently returned from London. We had the pleasure of seeing one of your lieutenants while we were there."

He rubbed his side whiskers. "One of my officers? Who was that?"

"Mr. Wickham."

Elizabeth felt Mary stiffen beside her. She looked past her sister to see Mr. Wickham leave Mr. Denny, Mr. Chamberlayne, and Captain Carter; he walked in their direction.

"Mr. Wickham?" Colonel Forster said with a loud cackle. "So that is where the rascal went off to. I should have known."

The rapidity with which Mr. Wickham crossed the high street, the dramatic salute he gave to his superior, and the depth of his bow combined with the sharpness in his eyes and the quickness of his smile added to Elizabeth's determination to discover his real character. That he had heard his name and knew he was the topic of their conversation was apparent.

Mr. Wickham's voice was rich with confidence. "Colonel Forster possesses the perception of a falcon. There is nothing that goes on in the regiment that he is not privy to. He keeps us officers on our toes."

Colonel Forster's chest puffed out at the praise.

Elizabeth's gaze flickered over to Mary, who considered Mr. Wickham with open disapproval. Elizabeth's immediate reaction was to check Mary's bold expression, but Mr. Wickham did not seem even to notice her presence. What was more, Elizabeth found she agreed with her sister's estimation of the soldier's character.

Empty flattery to his superior officer. And now, blatant indifference to a perceptive young lady who deserved more courtesy. Mr. Wickham's charming glow was quickly losing its sheen. But was he a barefaced liar? Elizabeth would test him out.

Smiling sweetly, Elizabeth asked the colonel, "Did you not send him on a special commission?"

Colonel Forster's face reddened, but he apparently was not the sort of man to admit he had not the faintest idea what Elizabeth was talking about.

She watched Mr. Wickham in her peripheral vision. His smile was gone. Turning to him, feigning innocent ignorance, she added, "That was what we were given to understand."

Mr. Wickham dabbed at his forehead and tried to smile. Not a trace of guilt was in his eyes, but that she had caught him in a lie was plainer than the red of his coat. There had been no commission. His foray into London had likely been made on stolen time. He had played her for a fool, certain she would not question him.

Well, she could question him now. A wicked sense of retribution had her lowering her voice as she addressed the colonel. "Do not trouble yourself, Colonel. We shall not press you in matters which do not pertain to us to know. Your secret is safe with Mr. Wickham."

Said gentleman's eyes widened, and Elizabeth saw the beads of sweat break over his upper lip before he wiped them away. It was in her power to make a great deal more trouble for him. One mention of him purchasing a gift for Mrs. Forster, and his military career would be over. She could ruin him for misleading her and so many others—for maligning Mr. Darcy's honor. She considered it, but she could not be so cruel.

Claiming the necessity of seeing his wife, Colonel Forster dismissed himself, his stride assured and his posture elevated. It appeared that Mr. Wickham would have little difficulty appeasing him. He would say that Elizabeth was a confused female, and that would be that as far as the gentlemen were concerned. They would drink over it and carry on.

But while Elizabeth would not humiliate Mr. Wickham before his superior, she still had a bone to pick with him. "You lied to me." She turned toward her aunt's, holding tight to Mary, not wishing to be in Mr. Wickham's company a moment longer than she needed to make her point. Was he the "friend" who had thrown the stone at the Great Dane, causing it to chase Mr. Darcy? Her pace increased the more convinced she became of the likelihood.

Like a scolded puppy, Mr. Wickham followed. She wondered how often he had used the downcast expression to garner pity. He would get none from her. Had he any honor, he would have apologized by now.

"Were any of your accusations against Mr. Darcy true?" she demanded.

"He refused me the living his father had promised me."

She whipped her head around to face him. "A living I must conclude you did not want. Would you have me and all of Meryton believe Mr. Darcy willfully went against the wishes of his father in an infantile fit of jealousy? Please, Mr. Wickham, you and I both know that is not possible."

Mr. Wickham squirmed.

Mary had been quiet all this time, so when she spoke, her voice was like a pistol shot. "A living under the patronage of a grand estate would be a blessing for a righteous-minded gentleman with good motive. Such a prominent place would provide well for his lifetime."

"Unless he sold his right to it," Elizabeth blurted, not imagining how true her outlandish outburst was until Mr. Wickham's complexion flushed a bright shade of red to match his coat.

So that was what had happened. He had sold his living. "Do you deny it?"

He did not.

In a flash, Elizabeth saw the depth of his betrayal. He—a young man who had been raised as Mr. Darcy's friend, admitted to being a favorite of Mr. Darcy's father, and given more advantages than the son of a steward would usually have—had sold his inheritance. He must have squandered the sum. Otherwise, why would he be in the regiment when he could have purchased a more prestigious rank in the regulars? And after benefiting from the Darcys' kindness, he had the effrontery to be bitter about it!

Mr. Wickham's smile was not so charming anymore. "When men like Darcy speak, the veracity of their claims is never challenged. A humble soldier has no hope of upholding his own honor under such persecution."

He was the victim now? Now that Elizabeth saw him clearly, she could only be disappointed in herself for allowing him to mislead her as much as he had. That stopped today. She would protect the people she loved from his influence. "I am not your enemy, Mr. Wickham, but I no longer wish to be your friend. Do not pursue my sisters' company, and I will guard my silence. Seek them out, however, and I will bring you to your knees."

He bowed his head, giving his word (for whatever that was worth), and walked away.

Mary smiled at her. "'Blessed is the man that walketh not in the counsel of the ungodly, nor standeth in the way of sinners, nor sitteth in the seat of the scornful.'"

"I have been a blind fool, Mary. How do you put up with me?"

"Love covers a multitude of sins," she replied pertly, making Elizabeth laugh.

Jane joined them at the gate. "How perfect to meet you here. I have a bit of a headache and had hoped you might return to Longbourn with me. Uncle Gardiner said he would see Kitty and Lydia home once his business with Uncle Philips is done."

Truth be told, Elizabeth had a headache, too. But her sisters were safe from the likes of Mr. Wickham now, and they had Mr. Bingley's return to Netherfield Park to look forward to, so she could not be miserable for long.

CHAPTER 24

Elizabeth was tempted to march into her father's book room and reveal her concerns, to beg him to be more cautious about allowing her sisters so much association with Mr. Wickham and the other officers. But what precisely would she say? That she had caught Mr. Wickham in a lie? That he was not sincere? The same probably could be said of most men.

Papa would listen with a gleam in his eye while he paid more attention to possible motives behind her change of heart than to the warning itself. He might even agree with her on some level before brushing off her concerns and doing absolutely nothing.

She needed proof, and she had none. All Elizabeth knew was that while she had once believed Mr. Wickham's story about Mr. Darcy, she now doubted everything he had ever told her. Was she being reasonable?

Were her conclusions merely influenced by her improved opinion of Mr. Darcy? Absolutely.

However, there had been Colonel Fitzwilliam's reaction at the theater. Elizabeth had observed nothing but open amiability from the colonel since her first meeting with him. But when Elizabeth had mentioned Mr. Wickham's name, the displeasure in his expression was too marked not to notice. A man who found every acquaintance agreeable did not like Mr. Wickham. Surely that added significance to Elizabeth's misgivings.

There was also the matter of the "special commission" Mr. Wickham claimed. Colonel Forster's blank expression suggested that no such agreement existed, but it was Mr. Wickham's blatant flattery to his senior officer that confirmed it. Why resort to flattery when he had been the one supposedly doing a favor?

Elizabeth was about to escape to the garden when her mother and sisters returned from Meryton in the carriage, bright-eyed with gratification and rosy-cheeked from adulation. Uncle Gardiner, they said, would follow shortly, his business with Uncle Philips taking longer than he had anticipated.

"Did you see how Captain Carter looked at me?" Lydia boasted as she tugged on the fingers of her gloves. Her rose petal pink kid gloves.

There was Elizabeth's proof.

Fury flamed in Elizabeth's cheeks. Did Mr. Wickham think she would not notice? He must have believed she was stupid when he had taken such a risk. "Where did you get those?"

Lydia preened. "They were a gift."

"From whom?"

Her sisters knew very well that they ought not to receive gifts from any gentleman to whom they were not attached. Such presents often came with certain little favors which could only lead to a lady's ruin. As negligent as Papa was and as permissive as Mama tended to be, their daughters knew that line was not one to be crossed.

Lydia tossed off her bonnet and replied saucily. "You are only jealous because you have no admirers to give you pretty things."

Mama spun around to face Lydia, then pulled her youngest daughter into her embrace. "Engaged! And so young! Which officer is he, dearest?"

Kitty howled. "I was offered a ribbon, too!"

"Hush, dear. These gloves are very fine indeed, such excellent quality. They must have cost the gentleman a pretty penny." Mama examined the embroidery, praising the evenness of the stitches and estimating their cost while Kitty's calls for attention increased in volume and Mary attempted to remind her younger sisters of the dangers of accepting such favors.

The commotion roused Papa from his book room. "What have we here?"

"Lydia is engaged!" Mama exclaimed, clutching the

evidence of the attachment to her bosom and tenderly caressing the soft leather.

"I am not engaged yet, though I expect an offer soon." Lydia snatched the gloves out of Mama's grasp and raised her nose at her beau-less, gift-less sisters.

Elizabeth wanted to shake her.

Mama's face fell. "What? Not engaged?"

Not a trace of humor or indifference softened Papa's expression. The pierce of his gaze seemed to fix Lydia to the spot where she stood. "Who gave these to you?" His voice was sharp.

Lydia stepped back, not so confident now that she sensed one of their father's rare reproofs. "I-I would rather not s-say."

"You will answer me." Father's steely tone brooked no argument, not even from senseless Lydia.

"Mr. Wickham." Lydia clasped her hands in front of her, her whisper echoing in the silent entrance hall.

Witnessing her sister's demureness before their father's punitive manner, Elizabeth wondered how different her sisters might behave had he exercised his authority years before. They might be spared this shameful conversation.

"What were you willing to exchange for such a fine pair of gloves?" he demanded.

Lydia bunched her chin, a weak attempt at defiance. "Only a little kiss."

Mama fanned her face and leaned against Kitty.

"Not engaged? We are ruined. All of my girls are ruined."

"And who else was present when this arrangement was made?" Father insisted.

Kitty became very quiet. So quiet that Lydia did not have to denounce her guilt with anything more than a flickering gaze.

"I see." Papa straightened his back, a solid wall that would not bend. "Have you exchanged any other favors besides this?"

Lydia shook her head vehemently. "Just the kiss."

Father took a deep breath, but his posture remained stiff. "Were you not aware that your indiscretion would have consequences?"

"George said he loved me—that we would marry."

"My dear girl, why would a man offer for an immature child when she is willing to sell her displays of affection for gloves? Did you not consider what he would ask of you next?"

"But he loves me! He wants to marry me." Lydia's voice quivered.

Mama wailed. "We are ruined!"

"It will be well, Mama. Calm yourself," Kitty urged.

"How can we be well when no gentlemen will have you now?!" Mama pushed away from Kitty. "And you helped her ruin us! How could you, Kitty?"

Papa held up his hand. "Silence. We do not know the extent of the damage done." Returning to Lydia, he dropped his tone. "Think hard. Who else might have seen you with that rake?"

"We snuck into Uncle's barn. Kitty stood guard at the door."

The muscles at Papa's jaw twitched. "Did anyone approach?" he asked Kitty.

Kitty's chin bunched. "Mr. Denny asked what I was doing standing outside the barn. I told him that Mr. Wickham was inspecting one of Uncle's horses. Wickham must have heard because, not a minute later, he came outside the barn flicking straw from his hair and straightening his coat."

Father's eyes drilled into Lydia. "One kiss?"

Lydia said nothing.

"Answer me, child!"

"It was only supposed to be one kiss."

Elizabeth went numb and cold. Mary crossed her arms around herself. Jane covered her mouth with her hand, tears falling over her fingers. Mama swooned.

Father pressed, "Was that all that happened? Did he remove any of your clothing? Any of his?"

"No."

"Why should I believe you when you have already lied to me about the kiss?"

Kitty rose to Lydia's defense. "They were not five minutes in the barn when Mr. Denny came."

Father's shoulders dropped. "Bless Mr. Denny. There might be hope for us yet." He asked Kitty.

"Nobody saw Mr. Wickham and Lydia leave the barn in a disheveled state?"

"Mr. Wickham left with Mr. Denny, and I went inside the barn to help Lydia fix her hair and—" She bit her lips together, her cheeks scarlet.

"And what?"

Kitty broke into tears. "And tie her dress. Only the top layer was undone."

Papa held out his hand. "Give me the gloves. I will return them to Mr. Wickham myself."

Mama lurched forward, clinging to him. "You must make him marry Lydia."

"I shall not! If nobody else knows of this indiscretion, I refuse to attach my daughter to a man who would use her poorly and cast her aside the moment a prize with a fatter purse or a prettier face appears."

Of all the things that should have made Lydia cry for shame or regret, it was her vanity which finally moved her to tears, for she had always believed herself to be the handsomest maiden in Longbourn and Meryton.

"You will challenge him to a duel, and he will kill you in the fields, and what will happen to us then?" Mama sobbed.

"I will do no such foolish thing, but I shall go into the village and ascertain how much damage has been done to our reputation. If the indiscretion is known, Lydia will have no choice but to marry the lout if I can shame him into it. If it is not, then I shall have to guarantee his silence."

"How?" Elizabeth asked.

"He will have debts. I shall pay them. But let it be known that no officer or gentleman is to set foot in this house without my express permission." He pointed at Kitty and Lydia. "There will be no more walks into Meryton until I can secure a proper governess. You will return to the nursery until you have learned how to comport yourselves in society without bringing shame upon our entire household."

"B-b-but B-Brighton! I have already agreed to go as Mrs. Forster's special guest!" Lydia stuttered.

"Shall I reward your brash conduct by allowing you to go to the sea? No, my dear, it is back to the schoolroom for you. You will not leave this house for the foreseeable future." Tucking the damning gloves into his pocket, Papa donned his hat and coat and was gone for the rest of the afternoon, leaving Elizabeth sufficient time to plan Wickham's downfall. She *had* warned him, after all.

CHAPTER 25

Darcy's impatience grew as the days leading to Bingley's return to Netherfield Park crept languidly by.

By Thursday, he actively questioned Bingley's insistence on waiting until Monday to depart. Darcy's arguments, while persuasive, were met with reasonable logic. As much as Bingley would like to quit London a few days earlier, the house was not yet ready to receive them. Nor was his business in town entirely settled. Not even Darcy thought it sound for Bingley to quit town only to have to return the following day.

By Friday, Darcy was in a pitiful mood. One moment, Richard sympathized with his ill-humor, and the next he badgered Darcy mercilessly. "Absence makes the heart grow fonder," he teased.

"Or makes the man unbearable," Bingley quipped.

Darcy glared at both of them. Richard's influence

on Bingley was insufferable. And yet, he would have to tolerate both of them at Netherfield Park—an annoyance he would endure a hundred times over for the promise of gazing upon Elizabeth.

Already Darcy imagined her smile, and his aggravations melted away until his irksome cousin and his pesky pupil cast him knowing glances full of false pity and suppressed humor, reminding Darcy of the source of his dissatisfaction—that he was stuck in London while Elizabeth was at Longbourn with Wickham circling around the Bennets like a red kite intent on swooping down upon its next meal.

In his dreams, Darcy rode into Meryton to the tipped hats and bobbed curtsies of the villagers he had scorned, his poor manners forgotten and forgiven in the wake of Wickham's exposed sins. Elizabeth will have found him out and, bold defender of her family that she was, she had taken measures to protect them.

By Saturday, Darcy threw caution to the wind and had his horse saddled with orders for his valet to follow him to Meryton's Inn in the carriage. He had ridden as far as Highgate Hill before sense caught up with him. His impatience would only lead to disaster. He must bide his time and wait for Bingley, who offered Darcy the perfect reason to return to Hertfordshire.

By Monday, Darcy's nerves would have rivaled those of Mrs. Bennet. Was Wickham still a favorite? Darcy could not bear to appear inferior to the scoundrel in Elizabeth's esteem. Wickham was undeserving of her good opinion. And while Darcy knew himself to stand on rather shaky ground in her estimation, he was determined to prove himself.

Driving past Longbourn to Netherfield proved to be an intense exercise in restraint. Darcy easily conjured half a dozen excuses to stop: surely Bingley wished to call on Miss Bennet, the horses were lagging and required rest or water, Ruby needed to stretch her legs, Darcy needed to stretch his legs.

In the end, he rested his forehead against the glass separating him from the tantalizingly short distance to Longbourn and Elizabeth, his only consolation the knowledge that, at this hour, Elizabeth was unlikely to be indoors. He would sooner find her walking through a field.

Though he looked for her figure strolling through the countryside—her bonnet dangling in her hand, her hair shining and her curls escaping from her pins—Darcy did not see her before the coach finally halted in front of Netherfield Park.

How soon could he call?

A snort from the seat opposite recalled Darcy to his senses. Richard shook his head. "You should look at you two. A couple of love-sick puppies!"

Darcy glanced at Bingley. Did he look as pathetic as that? Summoning a scowl, Darcy opened the carriage door.

After four hours inside the conveyance, he had little

desire to spend the rest of his day indoors. Neither did Ruby, who had slept most of the journey with her head resting on Darcy's leg, her drool seeping into his breeches.

Chalmers had another pair ready for him to don, and within a quarter of an hour of their arrival, Darcy had freshened up, changed out of his travel clothes, and was ready to take the animal for a walk. She pranced beside him, seemingly aware of the new collar he had had made for her with shimmering rubies arranged on a thick chain and held in place with straps of leather.

Unfortunately, Richard and Bingley met them at the bottom of the stairwell.

"Bingley and I had thought to walk into Meryton. Care to join us, Darcy?" Richard watched him too closely. "Or is there somewhere else you would prefer to go?"

...like Longbourn, Darcy completed in his mind. After a full morning of teasing comments and taunting looks, Darcy would not give Richard the satisfaction. Returning his grin, Darcy said, "There is nothing I would like more."

"More than our continued company? I doubt that!" Richard guffawed.

Pressing his eyelids together, Darcy took a deep breath and signaled for Ruby to heel. She stepped so prettily at his side, occasionally looking up for instructions as she did, that Darcy's heart swelled with pride. She was a clever pup and such a quick learner!

Boots crunched over gravel, and Bingley scrambled to catch up. "Have pity for those of us with shorter legs, man!"

Darcy glanced down at Ruby. "You are having no difficulty, are you, love?"

"If I had four legs, I would not have to trot to keep up with you," Bingley grumbled.

Richard caught up with them. "Children, children, we need not race. You shall only arrive at the village red-faced and smelling of your exertions."

Addressing Bingley, Darcy said, "Perhaps we ought to slow down for the old man."

They jabbed and jested all the way into Meryton. Though Darcy did not see Elizabeth along the way, he felt lighter than he had all week. So happy was he in the knowledge of their proximity, he gave up trying to assume his usual somber expression after several failed attempts.

Mr. Turner at the stables raised his hand in greeting. "Good day to you, Mr. Darcy!" he said, and he sounded like he meant it. Darcy could not recall ever exchanging a pleasant word with the man, and his surprise halted his step long enough for one of the stable boys to run over to admire Ruby.

"She is a beauty!" the boy exclaimed.

Ruby greeted him happily, tail wagging and tongue lapping at the lad's hands.

"And so friendly! How old is she, sir?"

If Darcy had never uttered more than the briefest

greeting to the stable owner, he had certainly never said anything to the stable hands. But the boy's interest in his pet was genuine, and Darcy was so eager to boast about her that he dismissed this breach of propriety.

"She is five months old. Her name is Ruby."

The boy extended his hand as though he wished to shake her paw, and to Darcy's immense satisfaction, Ruby rested her paw in the boy's hand. Clever girl!

"Blimey! Look at that! Such a polite dog is Miss Ruby!"

Bingley introduced Richard to Mr. Turner and his son, who also had the good taste to admire Miss Ruby. They had no sooner departed from the stables when the blacksmith greeted them. Then the innkeeper. Then the shopkeeper. And the butcher. And Mr. Philips, Elizabeth's uncle. Darcy bowed a little deeper to him.

"This is the friendliest village I have ever seen." Richard elbowed Darcy.

Bingley turned to Darcy. "They even seem happy to see you."

Richard snorted. "Friendly, but deprived of good taste."

Darcy was too bewildered to reply to Richard's gibe. Not even in his dreams had the villagers overlooked his abominable manners so thoroughly as this. What had changed?

Raised voices from the direction of the public house provided a welcome distraction and a potential answer to the unexpected turn of events. Wickham stumbled backwards out to the street as the barkeeper pointed him away. The harsh gesture changed to an enthusiastic greeting when the man spotted Darcy, Bingley, and Richard. "Now, them's the kind of gents I'm happy to serve in my tavern."

Wickham skulked away, shoulders raised and head ducked, and he disappeared around a corner.

Richard gasped. "Now, that is a gratifying sight. I have waited years to witness Wickham getting tossed out on his ear." He slapped Bingley on the back. "No wonder you were eager to return! Meryton's charm has no bounds!"

Darcy was in awe. Could it be? Had Wickham finally been found out? His spirits fairly soared as they crossed the village, greeting the villagers and stopping so Bingley could introduce Richard. Darcy paid attention to their names, trying harder to remember them and ashamed he had not done so earlier. He knew everyone in and around Pemberley. No farmer was too low for his attention. Why had he not extended the same courtesy to these people, many of whom worked Longbourn's land? What a fool he had been!

Children played with Ruby, and Sir William's gamekeeper even approached to inquire what plans Darcy had for her. "Only five months old, you say?" He rubbed his chin, his gaze following her lines and exceptional form. "She is a perfect specimen."

Darcy smiled to himself, keeping Ruby's secret to

himself because she *was* perfect. She responded so well to her signs, which Darcy out of habit always voiced, nobody was the wiser. So long as she did not get distracted and look away, no one would suspect she could not hear.

They continued along the road leading to Longbourn, and Darcy was snapped out of his reverie by a hissed whisper. "Psst! Darcy!" Wickham emerged from the shadows of a rundown cottage. He approached them slowly, lips pinched into a thin line, his head tilted defiantly—a picture of pride grappling with desperation.

Ruby growled, her tail still and her hackles up. Darcy patted her head, his own knuckles itching, his senses sharpening. "Good girl."

Wickham glanced between Ruby and Darcy, confusion crossing his expression before he settled on Darcy. "I find myself in a bit of a pinch. Could you loan me a small sum, Darcy? For old time's sake?" His clothes were wrinkled, his boots mud-spattered. Darcy wondered how long Wickham had been without a batman. He must be in dire straits indeed, if he could not afford to keep up appearances.

Richard crossed his arms over his chest, visibly restraining himself from inflicting bodily harm on the rogue. "You have some nerve!"

Darcy rested his hand on Richard's shoulder, both to calm his hot-blooded cousin and to express appreciation for his support. Addressing Wickham, he said,

"What I told you at Ramsgate stands. You are dead to me. If you think I will continue to cover your debts, you are deluded."

Wickham smoothed his cravat, his mouth twisted bitterly. "You are a resentful beast, Darcy. I humiliate myself to beg for your assistance, and you delight in my misery. It is not bad enough you denied me the living your own father bestowed upon me—"

"The living you sold for three thousand pounds?" Darcy asked, wondering if Wickham had told the lie so many times that he actually believed it.

Ruby made her disfavor known further with a low, throaty growl. Darcy kept the lead tight, but he did not pull her away. Let Wickham worry.

"How convenient of you to forget that detail," scoffed Richard. "You have no claim on Darcy. You sold your soul for three thousand pounds, and it is only by our good grace you were not shot in some nameless field outside Ramsgate."

Wickham's face turned red. His sins against Darcy and his family ran deeper than purse strings.

"B-but that does not excuse your contemptible behavior toward me. Not one shopkeeper in the village will extend me any more credit."

Bingley gasped. "You would accuse Darcy of acting dishonorably? How dare you, sir!"

It did Darcy's sense of justice good to have his friend defend him before the man who had charmed his way into the favor of the majority. This levity allowed Darcy to see Wickham the way Elizabeth would have at that moment, and he almost laughed at the irony of his foe's situation. "Your lenders are demanding immediate payment, are they?"

Wickham stepped away from Ruby, keeping a watchful eye on her. It would serve him right if Darcy let her loose but, tempting as the prospect was, he was a gentleman and he would not spoil the dog's palate with such rotten flesh.

"The colonel has me under guard. I can go nowhere, and the regiment leaves for Brighton in two weeks. How am I supposed to get by until then?" Wickham whined.

"And you had hoped to leave without paying your debts." It was not a question. Taking a deep breath, Darcy continued, "Answer me this: how are these families you owe supposed to subsist when men like you take advantage of their generosity?"

Bingley scoffed. "And he called *your* conduct contemptible!"

Wickham must have sensed that his prospects were nil. "You would do anything to ruin me." Panic made his voice squeak.

"You hardly need my help when you are perfectly capable of ruining yourself." Darcy shook his head, sad at all the wasted opportunities both he and his father had given Wickham.

"You ratted on me! It had to be you!"

Years of disappointment and hopeful patience

snapped under Wickham's accusation. Had he not learned his lesson after what he had attempted with Georgiana? He should be too ashamed to see his own reflection—wooing an innocent girl not yet out in society to satisfy his own greed!

Liquid rage pulsed through Darcy. "I have said nothing, a fact which I now regret. If I am to be accused of betraying your spendthrift ways and debauchery, I would much rather have done the deed than not. Understand me, Wickham, I will not hesitate to do so. In fact, I look forward to the opportunity." He stepped forward, and Ruby bared her teeth, watching Darcy for a sign to attack—never mind that was not a sign she had learned, nor would Darcy ever teach her something so barbaric. However, there was no mistake about it. She would defend Darcy.

Richard stepped between them. "How very sensible of you, Darcy." He coaxed Ruby back.

Bingley nodded his support, his frame puffed up to his full height.

Wickham turned to leave, but Darcy stopped him. He needed to know why all of Meryton had turned on Wickham, why everyone had been so happy to see him. It could not have been anything he had done, which meant… Dare he think it? Was this Elizabeth's doing? "When did this change come about?"

"This week. The past few days."

Bingley clapped his hands together. "That settles it.

We have only just arrived today, so it could not have been Darcy."

Wickham frowned, his eyebrows meeting before he retreated.

The one possibility Darcy most desired did not seem so far-fetched now. He knew it could be his undoing, but his hope soared. Elizabeth had proven herself trustworthy beyond his wildest expectations, and she had rewarded him a hundredfold.

He had to see her.

CHAPTER 26

After a morning of wistful thoughts, each one adding to Elizabeth's restlessness, she decided to enjoy the best of nature's beauty by walking to Oakham Mount. Unfortunately, she found the exercise was not settling her scattered reflections.

True to his word, Papa had wasted no time securing a governess. Miss Hale was the daughter of a highly esteemed gentleman Papa had befriended at Cambridge. The man had recently suffered a reversal of fortune when his partner had made off with all of their business assets, leaving mountains of debt for Mr. Hale and impelling his rational daughter to earn a living in the best way she could. Being an accomplished musician, she had intended to take on students until Papa's letter to her father convinced her that her accomplishments might have a greater impact for good in Hertfordshire.

Miss Hale (or Hannah to Jane and Elizabeth) was Charlotte's age, refined, too handsome not to have received many proposals, and too intelligent to accept an offer of marriage unless it promised to increase her happiness.

"Not marry?" Mama had exclaimed. "What of your future? Your security?"

Hannah had merely smiled and assured Mama (who was unconvinced any lady could possibly be happy unless she were married) that she enjoyed her own company too much to disrupt her peace with a gentleman. Besides, her lowered station was temporary. Her father would track down the criminal responsible for their bankruptcy, and then she would have to swat away unwanted proposals like pesky flies at a picnic. Consequently, Mama had expressed severe doubts about Hannah's qualifications as a governess.

Elizabeth was pleased that Papa had not been swayed. One firm decision carried out to completion led to more, and Mama's fits of the vapors were proving to be less effective and therefore might soon become less frequent. Papa, in turn, enjoyed the prospect of peace sprouting in his household.

Kitty looked at Hannah with something close to awe and followed her like a shadow. Lydia, having lost her most loyal disciple, had taken an instant dislike to their new governess. To the lady's credit, Hannah did not trouble herself over Lydia's childish rants and tantrums. She merely sent Lydia to her room to enact her outburst in solitude. Without an audience to witness her dramatics and not much enjoyment of her own company, Lydia's behavior showed the first signs of improvement.

And there was Mary. Elizabeth's heart was filled with elation for her sister who, in only two days of association, blossomed under Hannah's tutelage at the pianoforte. With gentle encouragement to read more poetry and to contemplate the praises of creation rather than the dry sermons and rigid messages in the pamphlets she liked to read, Mary and her strictly pious views might soften—such was Elizabeth's fervent hope. Art, Hannah said repeatedly, was a God-given gift one should enjoy as much as the thrill in a bird's song or the burbling of a brook or a child's laughter.

Yes, Hannah had indeed been a blessing to the Bennet family since her arrival, but Elizabeth's thoughts maddeningly continued to stray to Netherfield Park. Jane said Mr. Bingley planned to arrive early that same day. Would Mr. Darcy return with him?

There was so much Elizabeth wanted to tell him. She wanted to apologize. She had been wrong about Mr. Wickham and, as a result, she had been woefully unjust to Mr. Darcy. Elizabeth had believed him the worst sort of gentleman—cruel and without honor. How had he reacted? By trusting her.

Guilt gnawed at Elizabeth's bones. The least she could do was to assure Mr. Darcy his faith in her had not been misplaced.

She ran her fingers through the smooth ribbons on her bonnet, leaning her face back to let the sun warm her cheeks and melt the tension in her shoulders. Hearing a bark, she blinked at the shadows approaching, her breath catching in her throat when her vision adjusted to the light. It was Mr. Darcy.

Elizabeth knew she should temper her smile, but she was too happy to see him and Ruby.

Stooping down—though the animal had grown so much she hardly needed to do so— Elizabeth opened her arms for the puppy to come. Mr. Darcy looped the lead around the collar and let Ruby bound to her. The dog's greeting was no less enthusiastic than it had been at their first meeting, although she now sported a lovely collar with a ruby encircled with pearls resembling a flower, just like Elizabeth's own necklace.

Mr. Darcy blushed. Gesturing at the collar, he said, "Ruby's are paste and beads."

Elizabeth was shocked he would admit to allowing his dog to wear paste jewels, but she was learning that Mr. Darcy was full of surprises, so she teased instead. "How very kind of you not to curtail Ruby's diversion by burdening her with real gemstones."

"She could not brawl with geese or trample in the muddy banks of a river otherwise." The corner of his mouth quirked.

Elizabeth buried her face in Ruby's neck. She had so much to tell Mr. Darcy, but now that he stood in front of her, teasing and laughing, the words twisted and tangled in her mind. Where should she start?

The curl in his lips had spread wider. Was he happy to see her too?

She had only begun to hope so when his smile vanished. "I saw Wickham," he said.

"Ah, yes, Mr. Wickham's misfortunes have been great, indeed." Elizabeth released Ruby to stand. Glancing around to make certain that nobody would overhear, she said, "He came near to ruining Lydia."

She pressed on, unable to stop now that she had begun. She told Mr. Darcy about the gloves and their new governess. She described with pride her father's firmness, and how he had encouraged the shopkeepers to consult with each other to determine the extent of Mr. Wickham's debts. Apparently he owed everyone in the village much more than a soldier could ever pay. Much more than her father had been willing to spend on the wastrel.

Mr. Darcy threw a stick for Ruby to fetch. "How did your father secure Wickham's silence without covering his debts?"

"He threatened to expose Mr. Wickham's liberties with Lydia, thus forcing him into an unwanted marriage to an immature, penniless wife." Elizabeth grinned. She had been so proud of her father for not forcing such a union when Mr. Wickham and Lydia would have made each other miserable.

Mr. Darcy took off his hat, smacking it against his

leg. The muscles at his jaw flinched, a signal Elizabeth understood to reflect the intensity of his distress. "I am sorry. I should have warned you sooner, I should have—"

She raised her hand. "We both know I would not have listened. You judged my character correctly while I believed the worst of you. I am sorry."

He heaved a deep breath, and for several minutes they watched Ruby hop from bush to tree, sniffing contentedly and chasing early butterflies. Every so often, the Great Dane looked at Mr. Darcy as though to ask if she could continue to play. That was when Elizabeth realized that Mr. Darcy no longer smelled of bacon. What did he smell of now? Probably leather and shaving cream.

His voice jolted Elizabeth out of her musings. "I take no pleasure in Wickham's disgrace. We grew up friends."

Remembering Mr. Darcy's own words from the Netherfield Ball, Elizabeth repeated, "He is blessed with such happy manners as may ensure his making friends. Whether he is capable of retaining them is doubtful."

Mr. Darcy sighed again. "I meant to warn you."

She shrugged, determined that they eschew feeling guilt over a man who had proven himself unworthy of their consideration. "Had I possessed more discernment, I might have understood your warning, but I did not. Mr. Darcy, pray let us put this behind us. It is done. I believe we have both learned our lesson."

He held out his arm in a gentlemanly gesture Elizabeth accepted as a truce. Ruby followed, prancing and sniffing.

"Very well, but only if you will allow me to state again how sorry I am for my high-handed interference between Bingley and your sister. It led me to act unkindly. In addition, I see how your family's ignorance of Wickham's true character could too easily have led to ruination. It was inconsiderate of me to remain silent."

"I understand your reasons for silence regarding Mr. Wickham. He made friends too easily for any of us to believe you."

He pinched his eyes closed and sucked in a breath. "There is more." He spoke slowly, hesitantly.

Wishing to spare him from pain, Elizabeth squeezed his arm. "You need not tell me."

"He very nearly ruined my own sister. Georgiana was but fifteen years of age when he convinced her to elope with him. She believed that he loved her." Elizabeth listened in stunned silence as Mr. Darcy described the whole of Mr. Wickham's offenses against himself, his father, and his young sister. "I firmly believed I was done with the scoundrel, so you can imagine my surprise when he showed up in Meryton."

"That must have been dreadful for you," Elizabeth gasped. How differently that scene played out in her memories now. She had condemned Mr. Darcy for riding away, but now she admired his restraint for not trampling the ne'er-do-well to death. She saw Mr. Darcy in a clear light now, and she wondered how he had endured her company when she was so insistent in her blind prejudice. How awfully she had behaved toward him!

"I should have confided in you sooner," he said.

"How could you have trusted me with information that could cause your sister's ruin?" Having been so close to scandal the past week, Elizabeth was keenly aware of the repercussions to everyone in their family. Mr. Darcy would have been consumed with guilt had his sister's reputation been destroyed. Thank goodness it had not gotten so far.

His gaze seized her. "Would you have abused my trust?"

"No, but you had no way to know that."

His eyes deepened, and Elizabeth felt foolish for suggesting that Mr. Darcy would ever say anything unless he was absolutely certain of it. She could not fathom how he had accurately sketched her character when she had completely missed the mark with his. But he knew her—in some ways, better than she knew herself. That he would share such an intimate and censorious detail touched Elizabeth to her core. He trusted her. He always had.

As she looked up at him—his manners relaxed, his hair curling over the top of his collar, his lips parted—

Elizabeth realized how thin the line was between hatred and love. Now that the truth had demolished the arguments she had held against him, she could only gaze upon Mr. Darcy with the utmost respect and admiration.

She realized that her gaze had fixed on his lips, and her face burned at her turn of thought. Until she looked up to see that Mr. Darcy had been looking at her lips too.

He sucked in a breath and signaled for Ruby. "May I walk you home?"

Elizabeth muttered something she hoped passed as affirmative. Now that the thought had entered her mind, she found she could not dismiss the idea of kissing Mr. Darcy—nor did she wish to.

CHAPTER 27

Darcy's feet moved, but his gaze too often settled on Elizabeth's face to make the endeavor of walking successful.

He tripped. It occurred to him as he pitched and foundered that he should at least relinquish Elizabeth's arm. But he was loath to do so. Not only did he crave her touch, but her rather firm hold had, on more than one occasion, prevented him from sprawling forward.

"This path can be treacherous," she said, tightening her grip and settling that particular quandary.

Darcy took note of the smooth footpath stretched before him. Not one loose stone or tree root marred the perfection of the surface. He chuckled, his mortification appeased at her delicacy on his behalf. He glanced askance at her again, a risky maneuver, but well worth the danger to see the curl of her lips and the way her curls caressed the slope of her neck.

Darcy tripped again. Even Ruby looked up at him dubiously. Elizabeth bit her lips together, her eyes dazzling when they met his. "Tell me, Mr. Darcy, are the footpaths around Pemberley as precarious as this one?"

Where Darcy found the fortitude to continue to Longbourn without wrapping his arms around the lady and inhaling the scent of her hair while pressing his lips to hers, he did not know. The path proved too short to fully describe the glories of Pemberley and—to Darcy's immense joy—he made it to Longbourn's drive without compromising Elizabeth or tripping yet again.

They conversed contentedly, arm-in-arm, until an uproar inside the residence halted them in their steps. Where Elizabeth had been laughing and free from cares before, she now hesitated to meet his look. The contrast shattered Darcy's contentment, for if Elizabeth was miserable, then so must he be.

"I had best see what has caused such an upheaval." She pulled away from him.

He knew she would rather face her family without him there to witness it, but he could not leave her alone to face whatever trouble awaited inside. He hated how she assumed—and rightfully so, he thought to his chagrin—that he would allow her to face trouble alone when he would always stand at her side to support her.

She frowned when she noticed him following. It occurred to Darcy that, while his judgements about her family had been truthful, they had not been kind. In giving voice to them, he had not helped them alter their behavior in the least. He had only succeeded in hurting Elizabeth. He wanted to apologize… again. However, Elizabeth had already opened the door.

Just across the threshold, he saw the source of the cacophony. Miss Lydia, red-faced and soggy, wailed. "I was supposed to be the first to marry!" The lady who could only be the Bennets' new governess held her arm, pulling her down the hall. Calmly, her voice just above the volume of her charge's sobs, she said, "Once you have regained your composure, you may join us. I heard Mrs. Bennet call for cake and punch." The two retreated down the hall, where Miss Lydia tugged free of the governess' grasp and stomped up the steps.

Elizabeth folded her hands together and turned to him, the forced smile and heightened color gracing her cheeks feeling like a kick to Darcy's gut. The governess returned, and Elizabeth performed a polite introduction. "Miss Hale, allow me to present you to Mr. Darcy." She looked over her shoulder, where Bingley and Richard and the rest of her family were seated. "I believe you have already met Mr. Darcy's cousin Colonel Fitzwilliam and their friend Mr. Bingley?"

Miss Hale begged pardon for the scene, Miss Bennet drew their attention to the tea table, featuring a box of Bingley's favorite macarons, and Elizabeth eased everyone's discomfort with a wily retort before they joined the rest of their party. An impressive trio of capable ladies to behold. Darcy did not disguise his admiration.

Neither did Richard, whose gaping mug was marked with bold-faced wonder toward the skillful governess who had rid them of the child's outburst with a marvelous display of proficiency and firmness—the very qualities Richard most esteemed.

Bingley unclasped his hand from Miss Bennet's, reaching for her hand again once he stood.

And Darcy understood. Their felicity was too marked not to recognize what had provoked Miss Lydia's outburst. Miss Hale's comment about the cake and punch suddenly made much more sense. In a blink, Elizabeth was at her sister's side, embracing her and laughing.

Darcy, too, crossed the room to Bingley. While he drew the line at an embrace, he showed his pleasure with several enthusiastic slaps on his friend's back. "It appears that congratulations are in order. I could not be happier for you, Bingley, and you, Miss Bennet!" Darcy meant the words and also marveled at how quickly his friend had acted. "I turn my back for a minute, and you are an engaged man!" Another slap.

Bingley's face colored pink. "She said yes!" he blurted.

"And a good thing it is too!" Richard added, addressing the rest of the family. "Bingley was wretched before Miss Bennet made a most welcome reappearance in his life. As one of his friends, I must thank you, dear lady, for putting an end to his misery."

Miss Bennet's smile stretched from ear to ear, her blush deepening to match Bingley's. They were a fine pair.

Darcy squeezed Bingley's shoulder one last time. "I wish you both every happiness." When he loosened his grip, Bingley wasted no time returning to Miss Bennet's side on the settee. Ruby wiggled between Darcy and Bingley's feet, a strange bark howl escaping from her. Translating for them, Darcy said, "Ruby wishes to express her joy at your impending union."

After going about the room receiving pets and approving coos, the dog reached Mr. Bennet's chair and yawned. Wiggling under the furniture with her legs poking out at odd angles, she curled up and rested her chin on her paws, her eyes heavy.

Mr. Bennet chuckled. "All this excitement is tiring." He made as though to rise.

Mrs. Bennet clamped her hand over his before he moved more than a few inches forward in his seat. "Oh, no, you do not, Mr. Bennet! We must celebrate Jane's engagement!"

Miss Mary stood, announcing, "If it pleases you to dance, I shall play a merry tune."

Darcy remembered her last performance at the Netherfield Ball. Bingley must have remembered it too, for he swallowed hard.

"What a wonderful, thoughtful idea, Mary!" Miss

Hale exclaimed. "The piece you have been practicing would suit perfectly."

Miss Mary glowed at her praise. Had she not been wearing a yellow gown that reflected a sickly pallor on her complexion, Darcy would have described her as handsome.

Mrs. Bennet clapped her hands vigorously. "Excellent! Let us move the furniture!"

Miss Bennet fretted. "What if we wake Ruby?"

"She will not be disturbed by the noise. So long as we do not bump her, she will sleep." Darcy reassured her, thinking more highly of Miss Bennet for her thoughtfulness. Elizabeth added her assurances to Jane when she was not easily convinced, and Darcy smiled his thanks to her.

Mrs. Bennet pointed, and Darcy and Bingley did their best to move the heavy tables and chairs out of the center of the floor. Richard stayed near Miss Hale, who was consoling a fretting Miss Kitty.

"Lydia will be disappointed to miss out on all of the fun."

Miss Hale's reply was swift. "Expressing concern for others is the mark of a kind-hearted lady." Miss Kitty brightened at her approval, much as Miss Mary had done moments before. The governess continued, "Perhaps the sound of everyone enjoying themselves will encourage her to compose herself more expediently." Bobbing a curtsy, Miss Kitty promised to check on her sister and return before the second dance began.

"Mr. Darcy, not there! The table must go over here!" Mrs. Bennet instructed.

Returning his attention to the task at hand, Darcy did as Mrs. Bennet directed. By the time she was satisfied, Miss Hale had joined Miss Mary at the instrument. Bingley stood across from Miss Bennet at the top of their short procession. That left only Elizabeth and Mrs. Bennet for partners.

Tamping down his desire, Darcy bowed to Mrs. Bennet. "Might I have the honor—"

Richard bowed beside him, extending his hand to Mrs. Bennet. "Not if Mrs. Bennet would rather dance with a soldier."

Mrs. Bennet's delight doubled. "Oh my! Whomever shall I choose?"

Mr. Bennet appeared at her side. "Just like when I was trying to court you, my dear, with the hordes of gentlemen fighting for your attention. I am only grateful the colonel is not wearing his army coat, or I would not have a chance." He straightened and reached out to her. "Since he is not, I will press my advantage and hope that I might dance the first with my wife."

The warmth in Mrs. Bennet's expression gave Darcy a glimpse of the beauty which must have captured Mr. Bennet's heart. She accepted her husband's hand.

When Richard turned next toward Elizabeth, Darcy fairly shoved his cousin out of the way to ask her first. Richard laughed and Darcy knew how ridiculous he must appear, but he did not care. Nothing—especially not his bothersome cousin—would keep him from dancing with Elizabeth. That she looked pleased to dance with him made his embarrassment worthwhile.

Moving to the pianoforte, Richard bowed exuberantly. "Pray allow me the privilege of a dance, Miss Hale." The governess fingered the pages of music she had been ready to turn for Miss Mary, and even Darcy felt bad for Richard when it became apparent that the lady would refuse his request.

Miss Mary cleared her throat. "I have been practicing this piece for two days and do not require anyone to turn the pages for me."

"Then I shall be delighted, Colonel." Miss Hale and Richard took their places at the bottom of the line.

The dancing couples were too cramped for private conversation, but the confined space allowed for elbows and hands to brush more often than they would have otherwise. Darcy's feet felt as light as his heart, and he laughed when Mr. Bennet accidentally trampled on Bingley's foot and Richard took a turn a touch too exuberantly and smacked Darcy in the chest. The ladies performed perfectly, suffering no collisions or blows.

True to her word, Miss Kitty joined them in time for the second dance. Miss Hale replaced Miss Mary at the instrument so that she might dance, and Darcy was the first to ask if she would be his partner. He was glad he did when he saw how much his attention pleased Elizabeth.

By the third dance, Miss Lydia had properly composed herself. Only a red, swollen nose betrayed her earlier hysterics.

Darcy danced with all of the Bennet females before Mr. Bennet pronounced that he was tired and suggested that the gentlemen return to dine with them that evening, wherein they could all partake of the promised cake and punch.

Ruby was sound asleep. Very carefully, so as not to startle her, Darcy moved the chair partially covering her and wiggled his arms under her bulk, pulling her to his chest and pretending that her sixty pounds weighed little more than a feather. Another month or two and he would not be able to carry her. He held her tighter, rubbing his cheek against the top of her silky head.

Bingley walked on clouds all the way back to Netherfield. "She said yes! She said yes, and I have never been so happy!"

Darcy was happy for him too. As much as his arms presently burned, his heart burned even more to propose to Elizabeth. But he was not so insensitive as to propose so soon after Bingley. He would allow them time to celebrate their joy fully. Would a week be sufficient? Or a couple of days?

CHAPTER 28

Elizabeth wrapped her feet in her nightgown and tucked them up under her, her arms around her pillow. "Oh, Jane, I am so happy for you."

Jane smiled contentedly, then arched her brow. "Mr. Darcy is quite taken with you. His admiration was unmistakable. He could hardly keep his eyes off you at dinner."

Elizabeth squeezed the pillow to her chest, disguising her smile in its folds.

"It pleases you to receive his attentions!" Jane teased.

Burying her burning face in her pillow, Elizabeth peeked up at Jane. "It pleases me very much," she mumbled.

"I thought you did not like him."

"I misunderstood him, Jane. Mr. Darcy… he is a good man. Responsible, intelligent, quick to act—"

Jane rested her hand on Elizabeth's knee. "But is he kind?" she asked softly.

"Yes," Elizabeth declared confidently. "He is one of the kindest men I know."

"Then my own joy is doubled, and I shall wish you as happy as I am."

Elizabeth gasped. "You sound like Mama! He has not proposed." Although there were moments when she wondered if he might. At the theater, before Wickham had ruined the evening. At Hunsford Cottage, though she dreaded to think how she might have reacted had Mr. Darcy chosen that inopportune time to declare himself. What a disaster that would have been! She had not even liked him then and would have refused him in no uncertain terms. Thank goodness for Ruby's intervention.

Elizabeth would have a more favorable reply now… if he asked.

DARCY JOINED Bingley and Richard in the billiard room. Bingley was too overjoyed to sleep, and Richard had grown rather pensive over the course of the evening. He was plotting something; Darcy was certain of it.

"Jane thinks it is a good plan," Bingley spoke excitedly. "We shall stay here at Netherfield for another year, thus allowing her to be close to her family and me to be only a short distance to London. I found an estate in Bakewell—"

Darcy interrupted. "That is between Pemberley and Matlock!"

Bingley blushed and cleared his throat. "A strategic choice which Jane supports. She knows my character well and agrees that a year learning how to manage the estate here will be beneficial, but we will wish for long-standing trustworthy friends nearby when we purchase an estate and have a family of our own." He added hurriedly, "I will not make myself a pest, constantly asking for advice, Darcy. I have learned my lesson, and I shall seek Jane's opinion before I ask anyone else's."

"As you should." Darcy bowed. Bingley was wise to consult his betrothed, and Darcy had little doubt he would continue to do so once Miss Bennet became his wife if he was already having significant conversations with her about their future.

Richard leaned against his cue. "And Mrs. Bingley will wish to be near her sister." He winked at Darcy.

"I have yet to ask."

"You should ask Bingley how it is done. He did a marvelous job."

Bingley bowed deeply and Richard applauded.

Darcy rolled his eyes at the pair of clowns. "I do not wish to intrude on your triumph. Not for another week at least."

"That is kind of you, Darcy, but if you knew my Jane at all, you would realize that her sister's happiness would only increase her own. She is the most generous lady I have ever known." Bingley's gaze drifted off into the distance before he snapped to attention once again. "I could put in a few good words for you if you like."

"I do not need help." Darcy frowned.

Richard quipped, "You never do, but it could not hurt."

Bingley cackled. "I never realized it until now, but I have always sought help from others I consider smarter than me, while you never seek help from anyone, being intelligent in your own right." Yet Bingley was engaged while Darcy was grudgingly unattached. When he considered this, Darcy did not feel overly astute.

Richard howled with laughter until he was breathless, and Darcy guessed his cousin's thoughts ran similar to his own.

Proposing to Elizabeth had proven much more difficult than he had anticipated. But surely all of their misunderstandings had been cleared now. His interference with Bingley and Miss Bennet had been corrected to everyone's satisfaction. Elizabeth had herself discerned Wickham's true character, so there would be no more difficulties from that quarter.

Bingley bumped Darcy in the arm. "My offer stands. If you require any advice or encouragement, it would be my privilege to assist you however I might."

It was a kind suggestion, sincerely given. "Thank

you, Bingley. I do appreciate the thought, but this is something I must do on my own, in my own way."

Richard shook his head, stirring irritation in Darcy's chest. Unwilling to bicker with his cousin on Bingley's victorious night, Darcy instead chose to retire. The company in his dreams would be an improvement anyway. While he loved Richard and Bingley like brothers, they could not compare to Elizabeth.

RICHARD WAITED until Darcy's footsteps faded down the length of the hall. "He is so close, but I still fear he will ruin his chances with Miss Elizabeth if we allow it."

Bingley slouched over the billiard table, aiming at the cue ball. "I tried, but Darcy is stubborn."

"If only we could direct his stubbornness in the right direction. He needs to prove that he accepts Miss Elizabeth and her family and her circumstances… the lot of it—not only to himself, but to her. Otherwise high society will be relentless in using their differences to drive them apart."

"I would like to see them try!" Bingley stood upright. "Miss Elizabeth is clever enough to manage them. She never was intimidated by Darcy, no matter how churlish he behaved. I saw her put him in his place more than once. Caroline, too."

Richard believed it. He had witnessed the same at Rosings. "I do not doubt her ability. That is not the issue."

"Then what is?"

Taking a deep breath, Richard ordered his thoughts. "As capable and as bold as she would be, the strain of being under constant scrutiny, the cruel whispers, backstabbing comments, and blatant snubs… they would wear on the strongest of women." Even Miss Elizabeth.

"Surely society would accept Darcy's choice!"

Richard scoffed. "They would praise his selection, calling her a diamond whilst in his presence. No, they would never criticize her in Darcy's hearing. The damage will be done behind his back. The little snubs are the most hurtful, and there would be many of them." He gave Bingley a look. He, of all people, should know this.

Bingley lowered his cue to the table and folded his arms over his chest. "How could I forget? It was my mother's dearest wish to be accepted. She saw society's refusal to accept her as her own failure, but the fault was never hers. The taint of trade was too strong for Father's fortune to cover. Louisa's marriage to a gentleman helped, but Caroline's overreaching ambition too often puts both of my sisters in a bad light."

"Society is unforgiving, and they do not easily accept anyone born outside their intimate circles." Richard rubbed his fingers over the smooth wood grain rimming the table. "Society—my own family included, I hate to own—will refuse her entry into their circles, and Darcy's failure to understand how their clandestine disparagement affects his bride will be a source of strife. I would rather see them happy and forever in love."

"Why, Colonel, you are a romantic!"

Richard smiled. "Do not tell anyone. Especially Darcy."

Bingley pressed a hand over his heart. "You have my word."

"Good. Darcy has been my steadiest friend, and though he would deny it to spare my pride, I know how generous he has been with me over the years." A colonel's commission was not uncomfortable, but as the son of the Earl of Matlock, there were other obligations expected of Richard, each one a strain on his carefully allotted budget. Despite that, every month since Darcy came into his inheritance, Richard had found a little extra to lay aside for his future, which was carefully invested in the four percents.

Bingley was a picture of concentration, his brows pressed into a deep V. "So, Darcy needs to witness society's derision and defend Miss Elizabeth? Is that right?"

"The long and short of it. I had hoped the theater would open Darcy's eyes, but that blasted Wickham was too great a distraction."

"Understandably."

Richard rubbed his chin, thinking aloud. "Of

course, I need to find a way to arrange it in such a way that Miss Elizabeth does not suffer. That would not do. Darcy would have my hide, and rightfully so."

Scrubbing his hands over his face, Bingley asked, "How would you accomplish that? Who do you know in society who would travel here to confront Darcy about his choice of a wife?"

Who, indeed? If Richard could only devise a strategy to attain what he had described to Bingley, it would be his greatest work to date. Darcy aimed to propose in a week. Who was so obstinate and sanctimonious that they would see Darcy's choice as a personal affront on all things duty-bound and right?

The room went still, and Richard's pulse slowed to a dull thrum as an idea took root in his mind. It was bold—nay, it was audacious. If it did not work, it would be disastrous.

But if it did... If it did, it would prove the depth of Darcy's devotion. And what woman could not love a man who would defy society's strictures in her defense? Richard's fingers tingled; his senses heightened. This could be his most brilliant strategy *if* it worked—and that was a big *if*, replete with risk.

Then again, what scheme was devoid of risk? Great nations were conquered only when a leader saw beyond the peril and uncertainty to the gains. And Darcy stood to gain so much. If Darcy could marry for love and be happy with his Miss Elizabeth, then he would beat the odds. He would prove that felicitous unions were possible, that one could defy society's expectations, including his own family's presumptions, and come out victorious. And if Darcy could manage it, well, then Richard just might have a chance too.

He would write to his aunt Catherine that same night. If, in the morning, he still believed his interference would benefit Darcy and Miss Elizabeth more than it might harm them, then Richard would send his letter by the fastest messenger he could find.

He had one week.

CHAPTER 29

It was too early for calls, but being so newly betrothed, Bingley's breach of propriety could only be looked upon with approval. As Bingley's self-appointed chaperone, Darcy accompanied him and Richard with nary a sliver of remorse.

He had thought it insufferable to be separated from Elizabeth while in London, but it was infinitely worse being so near her and delaying his proposal. A thousand times over, Darcy convinced himself to forge ahead—that Bingley and Miss Bennet would not mind sharing their joy.

It had been three days since Bingley's proposal and Miss Bennet's acceptance. Three eternal days. Perhaps three days was long enough.

Elizabeth looked upon him with a tenderness and regard Darcy had not previously known. She was certain to accept his offer; he had only to ask. The morning was a perfect model of spring. Puffy white clouds dotted the cerulean sky. Birds perched on leafy branches while flowers budded and blossomed, perfuming the gentle breeze. Darcy's horse snorted at a butterfly fluttering past. Ruby would have chased it had she been there. Her turn would come after Darcy had given his horse some much-needed exercise.

He half-expected to see Elizabeth walking across the fields. It was an ideal day for it. Perhaps he would suggest a stroll around the pond. She would love the lake at Pemberley. She would love everything about Pemberley, and he would delight in showing his estate to her.

He could hardly wait to see her expression when he showed her his mother's jewelry boxes. They occupied a whole secret panel in the closet of the mistress' dressing room. Of course, Darcy would take Elizabeth to the jeweler's immediately upon arriving in London. His wife must have something uniquely crafted for her, something evoking the nature she so loved—sapphires and emeralds with pearls, perhaps. As well as new gowns befitting her raised station.

How proud Darcy would be to have her on his arm. Not that he wished to expose her to society so soon after their wedding. He would take her immediately to Pemberley, thus allowing them time to bask in each other's company while wagging tongues tired before their next appearance in town.

"Is that Lady Catherine's carriage?" Bingley asked, his unwelcome question interrupting Darcy's reverie.

Darcy's initial reaction was to deny his friend's observation as ridiculous. What in heaven would his aunt be doing in Hertfordshire, and at this early hour? But as his thoughts drifted from his dream-like ponderings to settle in the present, he could not deny that the carriage sitting in the middle of Longbourn's drive directly in front of the entrance door was, indeed, his aunt's.

A cold dread settled over him. Richard drew his mouth into a straight line, his voice strained. "What is our aunt doing here? And at this hour?" There was no reasonable explanation for it, which meant that her presence had no rational motivation and could only purport disaster.

Aunt's waiting woman sat in the carriage with the door open, twisting her hands in her skirts, her eyes fixed on Longbourn's entrance door. Whatever their aunt's business was, it would be brief.

Darcy dismounted and handed the reins to the perturbed groom, who was so tongue-tied he was unable to provide more information than the time of her ladyship's arrival, which was not ten minutes ago. Darcy marched to the front door, and the house servant showed him into the sitting room.

Mrs. Bennet fanned her face and fretted. She pulled away from Miss Bennet's side when he entered the room. "Oh, Mr. Darcy, thank goodness you are here! I cannot decide if I should invite her ladyship for tea or to dine with us this evening. She is a very fine-looking woman, and her calling here was prodigiously civil, for she only came, I suppose, to tell us the Collinses were well. She is traveling somewhere, I dare say, and so, passing through Meryton, thought to call."

If his aunt was inside Longbourn's walls, Darcy did not see her—a strange occurrence which only increased Darcy's vexation, for his aunt was not one to allow herself to go unnoticed.

Mr. Bennet interjected, "I dare say her ladyship would refuse any further offers of refreshment as impolitely as she did the first."

Darcy closed his eyes and pinched the bridge of his nose, but his shame did not abate. Mrs. Bennet's manners were rough, often vulgar, but she was a generous hostess and her hospitality was genuinely bestowed. Not having been raised as a lady, her manners could be excused.

The same could not be said of his aunt. She had no cause to behave rudely to the Bennets. "I apologize, sir, madam."

Mr. Bennet cut him off. "She entered my home with an ungracious air, requesting no introductions to myself or my wife and offering no explanations for her appearance. She insulted the size of our park, called our sitting room inconvenient, declined Mrs. Bennet's repeated attempts to please her, then opened the doors into the dining parlor and drawing room as though she were the master of my dwelling. It must have pained her to pronounce the rooms decent looking when her determination since crossing the threshold was to find fault with us and our residence."

"I am very sorry for my aunt's behavior. It is not to be borne." His aunt was not there, but Darcy's gaze scoured the room once again. Neither was Elizabeth present, and Darcy's stomach sank as the trail of clues led him to the only possible reason for his aunt's imposition. "Where are they?" he asked Mr. Bennet.

"My Lizzy will put her ladyship in her place." Mr. Bennet puffed his chest.

Darcy wished he could sink into the ground. "She should not have to."

"Come, join us in our *inconvenient* sitting room. We will drink tea and await Lizzy's return. I am certain she will have a worthy tale to tell." Mr. Bennet waved for the gentlemen to sit. Bingley and Richard obliged, but Darcy could not leave Elizabeth alone with his aunt.

"I would rather see if Miss Elizabeth requires assistance."

"Yes, I suppose you would." Mr. Bennet nodded and held his cup closer for Mrs. Bennet to easier fill. "You should find them conversing in the copse of trees on the side of the lawn. *A prettyish kind of little wilderness*." He chuckled at what must have been Aunt Catherine's description of the area.

Darcy dismissed himself immediately, grateful when he heard Richard's footsteps following behind him. They had reached the edge of the copse when Aunt's voice reached Darcy. "You are resolved to have him?" she demanded.

Holding his hand out to stop Richard, Darcy froze in place, a reaction borne from his urgent need to know Elizabeth's reply.

"I have said no such thing. I am only resolved to act in that manner which will, in my own opinion, constitute my happiness, without reference to you, or to any person so wholly unconnected to me." Elizabeth spoke boldly, firmly. She did not refuse. Darcy had hope!

"You refuse, then, to oblige me." Aunt's voice was sharp. "You refuse to obey the claims of duty, honor, and gratitude. You are determined to ruin him in the opinion of all his friends, and make him the contempt of the world."

Darcy clutched his stomach, feeling his aunt's rebuttal like a jab. He wanted to move forward, but he had no breath.

"Neither duty, nor honor, nor gratitude have any possible claim on me, in the present instance," replied Elizabeth. "No principle of either would be violated by my marriage to Mr. Darcy. And with regard to the resentment of his family, or the indignation of the world, if the former were excited by his marrying me, it would not give me one moment's concern—and the world in general would have too much sense to join in the scorn."

Elizabeth defended herself with the grace and

eloquence of a queen, but his aunt believed herself too far above her company to accept reason. When Darcy finally managed to force his feet forward, neither lady noticed as he and Richard approached.

"And that is your real opinion! This is your final resolve! Very well. I shall now know how to act. Do not imagine, Miss Bennet, that your ambition will ever be gratified. I came to try you. I hoped to find you reasonable; but, depend upon it, I will carry my point."

Heated with shame and anger, Darcy's voice shook. "You will do no such thing, Aunt. You have offended a family who has received you with the utmost graciousness despite your insulting intrusion. You can have nothing further to say. Allow me to return you to your carriage." He held his arm out.

His aunt took his arm haughtily, as though his gesture somehow proved her point. "I take no leave of you, Miss Bennet. I send no compliments to your mother. You deserve no such attention. I am most seriously displeased."

Darcy pulled her away from Elizabeth, looking over his shoulder at Richard, who immediately understood his unspoken plea and saw Elizabeth inside to her family. Darcy would spare her any more of his aunt's arrogant wrath, and he would ensure at this very moment that his aunt would take no such liberties in the future. Stopping, he faced her. "If you had any concerns regarding my future, you should have expressed them to me."

Aunt Catherine narrowed her eyes at him. "She has bewitched you with her feminine arts."

A scoff escaped Darcy's lips. "Miss Elizabeth has spent the greater part of our acquaintance disliking me with an intensity rivaling your own current displeasure."

"A trick! A ruse! She has taken you in so completely, you are blind."

"Kindly allow me to know my own mind better than you presume to." Darcy clenched his teeth.

"What of your family, your duty, your obligation to society and your name?" She tugged on Darcy's arm, pointing out every obstacle. "Your mother and father would be appalled! You shall be scorned by the very circles in which you were born. Think of Georgiana. You will ruin her prospects before she even comes out in society."

All the objections he had struggled with slapped Darcy across the face, refusing to remain unacknowledged or diminished. He was prepared; he had a plan to endure them. What he was unprepared for—what knocked him off his steady foundation—was the one thing he had not before this moment considered: the effect a union with him would have on Elizabeth.

Not once had he contemplated the inconveniences she would experience, for what lady would not wish to be the Mistress of Pemberley with a fortune at her disposal and all the accoutrements Mrs. Darcy would possess? How haughty he had sounded! No wonder

Elizabeth had loathed him! He had believed himself capable of giving everything advantageous and praised himself for overlooking her disadvantages, believing his condescension the epitome of gentlemanliness.

He handed his aunt into her carriage. "Have you nothing to say for yourself?" she hissed.

Darcy leveled his gaze at her. "Only this: I shall decide my future—not you, not my family, not society."

"And are you engaged to that—"

Darcy shot her a warning look.

"—girl?" Aunt amended.

"I have not yet made an offer."

Her eyes widened, and she clutched her heart. "You cannot possibly mean that you mean to offer for that… that—"

Darcy interrupted her before she insulted his beloved more than she already had. He could not allow it. "That is precisely what I intend to do. I can only pray that she will not hold my scandalous family against me."

Aunt sputtered before she found her footing in another insult. "Selfish boy! Your mother would be ashamed of you."

"My mother would applaud my choice." Darcy knew in his heart this was true.

"How dare you defile her memory! I do not know you. From this moment, we are strangers." Rapping her cane against the side of the carriage, she instructed her driver to continue to London. "Lord Matlock will hear of this. You will get no welcome from society if you dare attempt to introduce that hoyden to our circles."

Darcy stepped away, allowing the footman to close the door. He had nothing more to say to his aunt, nor did he wish to hear another word from her. He needed solitude, time to examine his thoughts.

But his aunt had come for blood, and he could not leave Elizabeth until he was reassured that her wounds and those of her family were properly mended.

CHAPTER 30

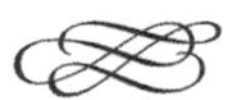

Upon entering the house with Colonel Fitzwilliam, Elizabeth sat between her mother and an empty chair, which he quickly claimed for himself. She wanted to bury her heated face in her hands and leap for joy. Instead, she clasped her hands in her lap and tried to make sense of what had just happened.

Lady Catherine had descended upon Longbourn like a hound on the hunt. Elizabeth's younger sisters had scampered upstairs like frightened birds—even Lydia had feared the woman enough to keep her mouth shut. Hannah had calmly followed them, but not before giving Elizabeth a saucy wink. She knew her ladyship's type all too well and was not intimidated. Neither was Elizabeth.

And good thing that was, for Lady Catherine had threatened and snarled. How much had Mr. Darcy overheard? Elizabeth's ears burned. He must have heard enough. He had defended Elizabeth before his aunt. He had chosen her.

She bit her lips together, trying not to smile when there were too many people in the sitting room who would notice. They watched her too, their expressions concerned. Elizabeth smiled at her mother, and then she realized what the topic of her chatter circled around.

Swallowing hard, Elizabeth hurriedly entered the conversation. "I hardly think Lady Catherine would be flattered to receive an invitation to Jane's wedding. She barely knows us."

Mama waved her hand. "How can you say that when she went out of her way to call on us only this morning? Such a fine-looking lady! With her as our special guest, we would be the envy of all Meryton!"

A cough escaped from the colonel. Mr. Bingley's eyes fixed on the floor at his feet.

Papa rose from his chair. "Now that it appears the excitement has passed, I shall return to my book room." At the doorway, he turned. "My dear, pray do not include her imperial ladyship in the wedding celebrations. I dare say she would not receive our hospitality with the graciousness expected during such a joyous occasion, and I would do nothing to distress Jane or Mr. Bingley."

He departed, leaving Jane, Elizabeth, and their callers to appease Mother with talk of lace and gowns and wedding cake. Colonel Fitzwilliam agreed with everything Mr. Bingley said, his gaze often traveling toward the door or the window. His leg bobbed up and down nervously.

When Mr. Bingley engaged Mama's full attention by offering to have the wedding breakfast at his larger property, the colonel leaned closer to Elizabeth. "I beg your pardon, Miss Elizabeth. This is my doing."

His unexpected statement befuddled Elizabeth. "What did you do?"

Just then, Mr. Darcy entered the room, his hair ruffled and his demeanor downcast. His eyes met hers, and the pain she saw in his expression made Elizabeth ache.

The colonel stood and bowed. "My apologies, but it appears that my cousin is suffering from a headache. I shall see him home."

Mama was too content making plans to protest.

Just as Papa had done, the colonel turned at the door. To Elizabeth, he offered an apologetic look, but he exchanged a somber nod with Mr. Bingley.

Elizabeth watched Mr. Bingley. What did he know? As soon as her sisters sensed that the danger was over, they piled into the sitting room, and Elizabeth seized her chance. Cornering Mr. Bingley, she said, "The colonel asked for my forgiveness but departed before he could explain why. Do you know what he wished to apologize for?"

He sighed. "I would only do my friend a disservice

should I attempt to explain. Richard's motive is pure, and his plans so rarely fail."

"Plans? Plans for what?"

Mr. Bingley bit his lips and winced as though he feared that was something he should not have said.

Elizabeth pressed. "Was he the reason Lady Catherine called today?"

Mr. Bingley blushed. "Oh bother! I have already said a great deal too much."

"Why would he send for her?"

"It was not like that. At least, it was not supposed to be." Once again, Mr. Bingley clamped his mouth shut, and this time Elizabeth knew she would get nothing more from him. He fled from her side, leaving her alone with her thoughts.

Why would Colonel Fitzwilliam inform his aunt of a possible attachment between Elizabeth and his cousin?

The answer was so obvious; Elizabeth could have smacked her forehead. The colonel was the son of an earl. Anyone born into such a position would take it upon himself to protect his family's position. Elizabeth had no claim on his loyalty, though she was disappointed to learn he was not the dependable ally she had once believed he might be. He did not think she was good enough for his family.

Her vanity ruffled, Elizabeth struggled to view the situation as the colonel apparently had. She was a gentleman's daughter, and Fitzwilliam—nay, Mr.

Darcy, she reminded herself—was a gentleman's son. They were equals. Except Mr. Darcy was the grandson of an earl. He had been raised in the lap of aristocracy. Elizabeth had no such claims. Nobody knew her family. She had no connections of which to boast. She had no fortune to cover over these deficiencies.

She leaned against the side of her chair, deflated. She was flattered to her core that Mr. Darcy had, at least at some point, made his favor of her well enough known for his family to concern themselves over it. But how could she forgive herself if he lost his standing in his own circles because of her? If she caused a rift between him and his family? What had she to offer him besides her heart? She had nothing he did not already possess tenfold.

Was she wicked for hoping she was enough? What of his sister? How would a marriage to Elizabeth affect Miss Darcy's coming out? Would she be received by her own friends? Her eyes burned and prickled, and Elizabeth excused herself. If Mr. Darcy could claim a headache, then so could she.

He would never do anything to disadvantage his sister, just as Elizabeth would never do anything to lessen her own sisters' prospects. His loyalty was one of the qualities she most admired. He protected the people he loved, and his family's hold over him was surely greater than anything she wished to presume.

Elizabeth walked down the hall in a daze, entering her room and sitting on her bed. She could not bear to observe him give up so much for her. She loved him too dearly. Her throat choked and her heart hurt—the desperation of recognizing that he loved her enough to rebel against society's expectations but that his family's demands were just too strong.

She buried her face in her pillow and mourned what might have been.

CHAPTER 31

Richard poured Darcy a drink, filling it to the brim. "Aunt Catherine is enough to drive any man to drink." Such as his uncle Sir Lewis who, in one of his drunken rages, had toppled off his horse to land on his head. Richard had many more thoughts on that particular subject, but that was neither here nor there.

His cousin had not said one word between Longbourn and Netherfield Park, and while Darcy never was one to waste words, Richard had hoped he might say something. Anything to distract Richard from the guilt churning in his stomach.

Miss Elizabeth had managed Aunt Catherine beautifully, but it had never been Richard's intention to test *her*. She would have tests and trials enough if she married Darcy. The test had been meant for Darcy.

No doubt, by now Bingley would have guilelessly

pointed the finger at Richard, the author of the plan-gone-awry. Miss Elizabeth would naturally draw the erroneous conclusion that Richard was against her when his only purpose had been to make Darcy a better husband. If they were to be happy together, Darcy had to understand what she faced. He needed to see that not all the sacrifices would be made by him—that he was not the prize he believed himself to be.

Richard had not planned for this.

Shoving the spirits at Darcy, he ordered, "Drink." Darcy did as he said without apparent thought. Richard waited, the air in the room becoming more and more difficult to breathe. What was Darcy thinking? Richard paced in front of the window, then he leaned against the fireplace mantel, but he could not stand idle for long.

Still, Darcy said nothing. Richard tugged at his cravat. This was ridiculous. Pouring himself a drink and refilling Darcy's glass, he sat across from his cousin. Like pouring spirits on an open wound, he would take a deep breath, grit his teeth, and wash this festering sin clean.

Deep breath. Hard swallow. Grit the teeth.

"You were right, Richard."

"Wha—what?" Richard had heard the words, but he could not yet comprehend them, so intent had he been on confessing his interference.

Darcy rubbed his hand over his face and through his hair. "If Aunt Catherine had any complaints, she ought to have spoken them to me. She knew I was at Netherfield. Instead she approached Elizabeth."

"That was unfortunate," Richard grumbled, rubbing his jaw.

"If my own aunt treats Elizabeth like a target for her barbs, what will society attempt? She defended herself courageously, but what will happen when her assailants multiply, amassing their attacks and waiting for the second my back is turned or the moment I believe her safe?"

Darcy covered his face with his hands and leaned forward until his elbows rested against his knees. Until that moment, Richard had always believed that a few casualties were justified if it meant winning the war. Seeing his cousin so thoroughly and profoundly undone… He could not justify it.

Again, Darcy spoke before he could. "I would fight them off, Rich. Every single one."

"I know it."

The door creaked on its hinges, and Ruby tentatively walked in, nose sniffing. When she saw Darcy, she hastened over to rest her chin on his knee while she looked up at him patiently. He absentmindedly stroked her head.

"They would be relentless. They would take delight in tearing my Elizabeth down, in spreading malicious gossip about her and deciding to despise her before she had the opportunity to display her charm, her intelligence. And I would hate them for it. I would come to hate my own family. You tried to warn me, but I refused to see."

Richard heaved a sigh, but it did nothing to lessen the guilt weighing down on his shoulders. Speaking through his tense jaw, he blurted, "I wrote to Aunt Catherine. I told her of your intention to propose to Miss Elizabeth."

"You did what?" Even Ruby reacted to the rumble in Darcy's thunderous tone.

Accepting his cousin's deserved wrath, Richard pressed on. "I suggested she call here to talk to you. I made certain she knew you were here at Netherfield Park. I made no mention of Longbourn or any further mention of Miss Elizabeth." Feeling lighter, Richard took in another breath, saying on the exhale, "I did not plan for Aunt to travel here so quickly."

"This was one of your plans?" Darcy sputtered. "You interfered purposefully, exposing Elizabeth to the censure of the world and the derision of a society I have never attempted to please." He fell silent as violently as his outburst had begun.

Pressing his fingers against his temples, Darcy groaned, "Just like I did to Bingley." He looked toward the door, as though he wished Bingley would walk through it and he could apologize once again for the misery he had caused his friend.

Richard could not allow Darcy's guilt to exceed his own. "I am sorry, Darce. It was never my intention to expose Miss Elizabeth to Aunt Catherine's ire. Our aunt was supposed to face you directly, to make you see what your bride would have to endure as your wife."

Darcy's shoulders visibly dropped. He shook his head. "I had thought to give Elizabeth everything: jewels, gowns, carriages, my undivided love. I could see no disadvantages to her when I magnanimously overlooked the deficiencies from her family, her lack of connections and fortune." His laugh was as bitter as his words. "I gave no consideration to what she would have to endure—the gauntlet she would face every single day until society grew tired of her or someone else provided a better target for their vitriol." He added quietly, "I cannot even rely on my own family to be kind to her."

Richard frowned. "I had hoped for better from Aunt Catherine. Believe me, Darcy, it did not occur to me that she would flaunt propriety so blatantly and make such rude demands behind your back. I cannot apologize enough."

Darcy ruffled Ruby's ears, his laugh less bitter. "Not long ago, I was in your position in Bingley's parlor. I needed his forgiveness, but I was convinced our friendship was through after what I had done." He shook his head and at least did not frown at Richard when he looked up. "I could no more deny you forgiveness than Bingley could deny me. I understand your motive was well meant."

The elephant stepped off Richard's chest, and he

finally breathed. "Thank you, Darce. If it is any consolation, I am on your side. And I aim to help you win Mother and Father over to your cause. I just… I wanted you to really be happy."

Darcy nodded. "I was prepared to fight for Elizabeth—I still am. Only now I have a better knowledge of the battle we will have to fight. I must acknowledge the sacrifices she would be forced to make… should she agree to be my wife."

It pained Richard to see Darcy doubtful, but after Aunt Catherine's rude display, Richard could not be so quick to offer reassurances. He kept his reply as neutral as he could. "If she loves you as much as you love her, she will count it an honor to fight at your side."

Bingley burst into the room. Between puffs of breath, he asked, "What… have I… missed?" He collapsed into the nearest chair, and Ruby trotted over to greet him.

Richard could not help it. "You do know you ride atop the horse, not run in front of it?"

"Ha ha," Bingley replied dryly. "You have no idea how anxious I have been since you left me alone to answer Miss Elizabeth's questions."

Richard groaned. "Does she hate me now?"

Bingley twisted his face. "Maybe? Quite likely?"

Darcy interrupted their speculative banter. "You are a good friend, Bingley. As are you, Richard… bungled strategy aside." He shifted his weight in his chair and clasped his hands together, his thumbs twiddling. "I find myself"—he cleared his throat—"in need of your help."

Richard saw Bingley's jaw drop, so he exerted himself to hold his in place. This was a moment to savor—Fitzwilliam Darcy asking for help. They must have missed their cue to say something because Darcy's frustration was audible. "How do I tell Elizabeth how I feel?"

Bingley considered for a moment, then shrugged. "I just said the first thing that popped into my head."

It was clear that was not the reply Darcy sought.

Richard added, "I have no advice to offer, never having been in love—"

"Not for long, I suspect," Bingley mumbled, adding in response to Richard's glare, "I saw how you look at Miss Hale."

Richard struggled to keep his composure, a feat accomplished by feigning a cough and distracting his companions from the deepening color of his complexion by pouring himself another drink.

Bingley, oblivious to the effect his words had on Richard, added, "Brilliant idea! Pour me one too, will you?"

When all three had their glasses, Bingley raised his. "To love. May each of us be blissfully happy with the women we choose to spend the rest of our lives with."

Richard agreed wholeheartedly, so he raised his glass. As did Darcy.

After they drank and the trail of fire down their

throats cooled, Darcy broke their contemplative silence. "How do I propose? What do I say? Must I kneel? And for heaven's sake, what do I do with my hands?"

Bingley splayed his hand over his chest and looked about him. "Me? You ask me for advice?"

"I am in earnest. I can think of no gentleman better qualified to advise me than you, who have achieved what I have only imagined in my dreams."

Bingley looked at Richard, the plea in his eye begging Richard to tell him what to say extinguished by the unhelpful response of a blink and a shake of the head. Returning to look at Darcy, Bingley replied firmly, "I believe we have interfered enough. Just tell Miss Elizabeth how you feel. Pour your heart out to her, and let her decide what to do with it."

"What if she refuses?" Darcy whispered.

"It is a risk you must take. But if you never ask, is it not the same as a refusal?"

Richard rubbed his chin. He had not expected such profundity from Bingley. It seemed that Miss Bennet brought out the best in his friend, and Richard could only hope that when his time came, a good woman would have the same effect on him.

Darcy felt as though he had been thrashed thoroughly at Gentleman Jackson's, and Elizabeth was the only nurse who could heal him.

He had to ask. He wanted Elizabeth to say yes so badly, but would she be willing to face all the families whose daughters he had snubbed over the years? She would have so many opponents who had nothing better to do but scrutinize her and criticize her while they sipped tea in their comfortable parlors.

Standing, he signaled for Ruby to walk beside him. She jumped and spun in circles when he pulled her lead out of his pocket and tied the leather around her collar. "You were there at my first attempt, and I wish for you to be there at my last."

Richard sprung out of his chair. "Right now?" at the same time Bingley exclaimed, "You are going right now?"

"There is no time like the present." Darcy sounded braver than he felt. He hoped the trembling would work out of his limbs by the time he reached Longbourn.

Half an hour later, Darcy stood at the entrance of the narrow gravel drive to Longbourn, his nerves increasing with every blink.

CHAPTER 32

"Lizzy, you have a caller." Jane handed Elizabeth a handkerchief and tried not to look dismayed at the wreck of her sister's hair.

Elizabeth sat up and sniffed. "I am in no condition to see anyone."

"You will want to see this caller, I think." Jane bravely attempted to smooth the worst tangles of Elizabeth's hair.

"With this red, swollen nose?" Elizabeth scoffed. "I would rather no one be so unfortunate as to see me in this state."

Her sister poured some water onto the cloth by the washbasin. "Here, press this against your face while I see to your hair. I wish we could change your gown for a nicer one, but we do not wish to keep your caller waiting."

"It is not Lady Catherine again, is it?" Elizabeth asked in a mixture of shock, panic, and bravado, remembering how she had been urged to change into her finest gown to be received by Great Lady herself in her Grand Parlor at Rosings.

"I should like to see her try to get past her nephew!" Jane chuckled.

Elizabeth hardly dared to hope. "Colonel Fitzwilliam?" she asked, wishing not.

Jane rolled her eyes. Although she did so in a kindly fashion, Elizabeth could not recall having ever inspired an eye-roll from her most forbearing sister. "Who do you think, silly?"

"You are in a humorous mood," Elizabeth mumbled, hardly feeling her sister's exuberance appropriate, given the circumstances.

Looking at Elizabeth askance, Jane said coyly, "He looks as miserable as you, if I may say so."

Fitzwilliam was here? Again? Elizabeth's heart stirred. "He looks miserable? Mr. Darcy?"

Jane grinned. "As miserable as I have ever seen him."

Elizabeth did not know what it said about her character that his misery made her own more bearable. (Nor about Jane's, since she seemed just as pleased.) But she dutifully held the cool cloth to her face while her sister soothed and cajoled her hair into place and fussed over her ribbons.

It did not occur to Elizabeth to be nervous until her boot hit the bottom step. What if Fitzwilliam bore bad news? What if he meant to leave Hertfordshire again? What if his sister had fallen ill? What if his aunt had suffered an accident in her haste to leave? (Not that Elizabeth held that lady in any tender regard, but neither did she wish any danger to befall her.) What if Fitzwilliam had determined that a union with her would bring on too much trouble? What if he agreed with his aunt?

Her stomach roiled, and her step slowed as she neared the sitting room. She listened for a reassuring laugh or a humorous tone, but she only heard low, somber voices. Oh, would that her mother were in the room! Her nerves were not always an accurate meter of emotion, but she was so consistently loud, she would have hinted to Elizabeth whether she should be heartbroken or excited. Once she crossed that threshold, her dreams would either crumble or come true.

Folding her shaking hands together, she stepped inside the room. She would face her fate like a lady, with her heart in her throat and her composure under strict regulation.

Fitzwilliam jumped to his feet as soon as he saw her, his gaze gripping hers until he must have remembered to bow, which he did awkwardly, nearly tripping over Ruby, who imitated his every move as well as a gawky puppy could. His nerves calmed Elizabeth, and she smiled at him.

"I apologize for my aunt's behavior," he uttered, as

though he had been holding the words in his lungs a great while.

Papa chuckled. "It was an... experience." He waved his hand and patted his leg when he caught Ruby's attention.

"Maybe so, but it was an experience you should have been spared."

Wishing to ease his mind, Elizabeth teased, "Mama has already gone to Meryton so she might boast about our highborn caller. Lady Catherine's insults could not have been received by a more grateful audience."

He did not laugh. "I am sorry."

"You did not insult me..." her thoughts jumped back in time to the Meryton Assembly, his disdainful snubs and fault-finding stares flashing through her mind in an instant. My, how he had changed, standing before her, head bowed, hands clasped in front of him just as hers were. So repentant. So humble.

While it spoke well of his character, she felt it necessary to tease him. "... not today anyhow."

That earned the smallest twitch of his lips. "Still, my aunt's appalling behavior reflects poorly on her relatives, and I do not wish for you to think for a moment that I shall tolerate such behavior. Not from her. Not from anyone."

"Yes, well, all of us have ill-mannered relatives by whom we pray we are not judged." Papa said what Elizabeth dared not mention with him sitting in the room. "Unfortunately, they tend to be the loudest and therefore draw the most attention." He looked down at Ruby and cooed, "Unlike this young lady, who may be a guest in my home any time she wishes." He scratched under Ruby's chin, and she leaned into him so hard his chair creaked.

Fitzwilliam smiled proudly. "Ruby is an exceptional student."

"She has a good teacher," Papa countered.

"Thank you, although some might argue that I conduct myself better with canines than with people."

Elizabeth's smile spread. Fitzwilliam was laughing at his fault? How delightful!

"Do you think perhaps," he continued, "Miss Hale would agree to spend some time at Rosings when she is through here?"

Elizabeth laughed along with her father. While Hannah's time with them had been short, she had worked some noticeable miracles. And Mr. Darcy had noticed.

Strangely, his ability to joke did nothing to relax his shoulders from his ears or still his hands from picking at one coat sleeve and then the other before gripping them together again. He swallowed hard and opened his mouth to speak, then met Elizabeth's eyes and seemed to forget what he had been about to say. "Do you—Would you—" He grimaced. Another hard swallow. A deep breath. "It is a lovely day." He pinched his eyes closed and sighed the sigh of a man who felt foolish for stating the obvious when he was more accustomed to being revered for his intelligence.

Elizabeth wanted nothing more than to kiss the dear man and put him out of his misery. If Fitzwilliam wanted her kisses. What if he did not? Her nerves increased, soon matching his own at the possibility that he might not want such displays of affection from her when she was so willing, so desirous of giving them.

Whatever Fitzwilliam wished to say, he was having no success saying it in the sitting room. And Elizabeth would have no indication of his inclinations until he did. She suggested, "It is a fine day for a stroll in the gardens."

"It is. Would you care to join me?" He held out his arm, then colored and turned to Papa. "That is, if Mr. Bennet approves. Ruby will accompany us."

So mannerly and proper, complete with a canine chaperone. Elizabeth turned to her father, expecting a sarcastic retort. She did not expect his gaze to fall on her, to feel the tenderness of his expression as her father's eyes blurred with moisture. He turned away abruptly and nodded to Mr. Darcy, and Elizabeth understood he had given his consent for something much more than a stroll in the garden.

CHAPTER 33

Darcy bowed his head, trying to communicate without presuming that he would take the utmost care of Mr. Bennet's favorite daughter… if she agreed to become his wife.

Elizabeth wrapped her hand around his arm, and he pressed it closer to his side before the intimacy of the gesture occurred to him. Surely this was an encouraging harbinger of what was to come… Darcy hoped. Already his throat was dry, his tongue thick.

Mrs. Bennet arrived in the carriage before they slipped away from view. Ruby barked, her eyes trained on the wheel spokes twirling temptingly toward them. Darcy quickened his pace, and Elizabeth kept up splendidly. It was too much to hope that they could escape from Mrs. Bennet's notice. The matron could smell an unmarried gentleman of fortune better than his hounds could sniff out a fox.

"Mr. Darcy!" She waved from the carriage.

He sighed, good manners dictating that he acknowledge her greeting when he dearly wished to ignore it. He made to turn, but Elizabeth prevented it. Under her breath, she said, "Keep going or you will hear of nothing but weddings and cake and lace for a quarter of an hour."

Darcy hardly needed more persuasion than that. He gladly followed Elizabeth's pace. "Will she not think me rude?"

"She will be flattered that you were so enraptured with my company, you did not hear her." She laughed as though what she said was not entirely the truth.

The pond descended from a gentle slope at the side of the house in full view of the windows in the sitting room. Close enough to see figures hovering around the glass but far enough that a conversation would not be overheard unless it was shouted.

Several ducks floated past, creating ripples in the water. On the other side of the pond, a gaggle of geese waddled around a grassy area which must have served as their nesting ground. The ducks stayed clear of the spot, and Darcy kept a watchful eye on them. Ruby, however, had not yet outgrown her belief that every creature she saw was her friend. She pulled against her lead, tugging and jerking as she hefted her increased weight in the direction she wished to go. He should have left her inside the house.

"Why do you not allow her to explore a little?" Elizabeth suggested. "She might make some new friends at the stables. Clarice does not usually like company, but she is accustomed to being around other animals. She will not harm Ruby." She nodded at the building to the left of the pond. A mule brayed in the paddock, and Ruby wagged her tail eagerly, tossing her head back to look at Darcy with a spirited request for permission.

Tying her lead around her collar and tugging it firmly secure, he motioned for Ruby to go. She trotted a few paces, then looked over her shoulder once more, bolstering Darcy's confidence that she would not stray too far. "Go!" he motioned again. "Play!"

Convinced she had approval, Ruby lumbered over to the paddock where the mule flicked its ears and watched Ruby hop between the poles of her enclosure. The two sniffed at each other before they began a game of tag.

Elizabeth pulled him closer to the pond. "Ruby has charmed Clarice. She usually chases the other animals away."

The ducks swam toward them, quacking for crumbs. The geese must have been accustomed to receiving table scraps too, for they soon joined them. Darcy knew their nest was on the other side of the pond, but he still backed away.

"You do not care for a swim in the pond?" she teased, pulling a piece of bread he had not noticed out of her pocket. Tearing it apart, she handed him half.

He rubbed his arms at the memory, the hair on his

skin rising painfully. "I am still recovering from my last encounter with their London relatives." They smiled at the shared remembrance, and for some minutes they tossed bits of bread to the greedy fowl. It was a peaceful setting, but the turbulence of Darcy's thoughts increased with each passing second.

Bingley had said the first thing to pop into his head. The trouble was that there were a great many things popping around in Darcy's mind, and he sensed that none of them were quite right.

The bread was slowly disappearing from his hand, and the pieces he threw became smaller and smaller. He had to say something before it was gone and he had no reason to claim more of Elizabeth's time. Would she refuse him if his proposal was pathetically imperfect? Would she accept out of pity? He did not want that.

Taking a deep breath, he tried to speak what was in his heart. "There is something I wish for you to know… a question I must ask." His heart raced, and he gulped his nerves down (only to have the dogged pests rise again). Bingley had made this sound easier, enjoyable even. Darcy thought he might be sick as Elizabeth looked at him expectantly. Her brown eyes were as dark as the night sky, the sparkle in them reminding him of stars. Blast Bingley and his useless advice.

Darcy cleared his throat, choking the words out. "I know my manners have been abominable toward you, toward your sister, your family." He swallowed hard again. This was not going well.

Elizabeth's eyebrow arched upward and her lip quirked. "You forgot the entire female population of Meryton and several of our families," she said with a saucy grin that loosened fear's chokehold on Darcy.

He looked down, catching his breath and calming his heart, returning his gaze to her with a smile he hoped looked genuine when he had yet to ask the question which would either lead to the greatest elation or the worst disappointment of his life.

More seriously, she added, "And yet, you have managed to secure the forgiveness of everyone in the village, Jane is engaged to a more decisive Mr. Bingley, and I—"

She paused, and Darcy held his breath. She what? The fate of his future hung in the balance, and his lungs screamed for air. And she, a lady who had never had trouble expressing her thoughts as quickly as the snap of a whip, had paused.

Elizabeth bit her bottom lip and blushed, and Darcy instantly forgave her hesitation while he attempted not to grant her demureness too much significance. He had mistaken her manners toward him before—confusing her passionate debates for something more intimate when she really had just despised his company. He refused to commit the same error again, though his heart flipped and tripped in his chest, traitorous organ that it was.

Finally she spoke. "I have learned that I ought not

be so quick to jump to conclusions about people. You are not the man I once believed you to be."

Darcy frowned. "What did you believe me to be?" He could have kicked himself for asking when he already knew the answer. Only a fool would ask her to expound on his worst qualities at a time like this.

He glanced over at Ruby, who still ran in circles with Clarice.

Elizabeth caught his gaze as he returned it to her. With a smile, she answered, "Proud men do not overcome their own prejudices (especially when they are admittedly deserved) to rescue unwanted puppies. Nor do they apologize and make amends when a mistake is pointed out to them. Therefore I must conclude that you are, in fact, both kind and humble."

His relief to hear her improved opinion manifested in a barkish laugh. But there was more, and he needed her to understand before he dared ask her to be his wife. "My family has always occupied a prominent place in social circles. They do not easily accept anything or anyone who challenges their expectations or threatens their place."

Elizabeth looked askance at him. "And yet you are friends with Mr. Bingley, and you have dined with my family… even those actively making their living in trade. Lady Catherine would be sorely displeased."

While Darcy appreciated her humor, these were issues that could not always be laughed away. "Your family is genuine in their hospitality, sincere in their expressions."

"No matter how garish?" Her eyebrow rose again, challenging him.

"After what my aunt did, can you still believe me capable of reproving your mother? Mrs. Bennet was not raised as a gentleman's daughter as my aunt was, and I have never observed her being cruel. I cannot claim the same of my family. They reflect society's norms, and society is often harsh. They would sooner cut a person behind their back than allow them a chance to prove themselves."

Elizabeth lifted her chin in that defiant manner she had that warmed Darcy's blood. It took all his restraint not to close the distance and crush his lips against hers. "I hope I never give them more credence than they deserve, which is very little." Her eyelashes lowered, as did her tone. "Is there any other deficiency you wish to claim? So far, we have covered your family and connections. Does your fortune also put you at a disadvantage?"

He laughed. "I do not trust easily, and I have lost more friends over money than I suspect most of the working class lose in a lifetime."

"How will you ever manage with such dismal prospects? At least they are not as bleak as mine—a lady with no connections at all, no fortune to speak of, and a family who is improving but who will never be welcome in higher circles."

"Would you want my connections if I shared them with you?"

She smiled. "That, sir, depends entirely on you."

"Will you allow me to share my fortune, my friendship with you? Welcome your family at Pemberley if you agree to endure mine? Weather society's cuts until our happy union makes a mockery of their taunts? I love you, Elizabeth. I love you with an intensity that burns my soul. It has grown stronger since the day I first realized the danger you posed to my heart." The words poured out of him, and he only just remembered to drop to his knee before he asked the question properly.

He did not remember when her hands found his, but he clasped them tenderly between his own. "Please marry me. I shall fight for you every day and consider the battle a worthy one if I can make you happy." He had not meant for his offer to sound so much like a plea, but if it meant Elizabeth would consider him, he would beg.

A smile spread up her face, brimming in her eyes and twinkling.

Darcy thought his heart would burst from his chest as he waited for her reply. She opened her mouth, one hand pulling free of his grip to caress his cheek... and a deep rumbling bark and the clatter of poles made Elizabeth turn and Darcy rise to his feet in time to see Ruby bounding toward them, her lead trailing behind her and Clarice chasing her outside the broken paddock fence.

Elizabeth gasped. "Clarice has never done that before! She generally aspires to my father's views about work."

Ruby raced toward them, and Darcy braced himself. She was too big and still too clumsy for her impact not to be significant. Dodging to the side to alter her course and prevent her from crashing into Elizabeth, Darcy grabbed her lead as Ruby brushed past. He held the leather tightly, trying to get her attention, but Ruby ran a circle around him and Elizabeth, pulling them together. It was Hyde Park all over again.

Clarice trotted around them, and the ducks and geese seemed intent on adding their quacks and hisses to the melee.

It was a ridiculously unromantic scene. Darcy laughed and held Elizabeth close to keep them both from tumbling into the pond.

Mrs. Bennet clapped her hands and squealed in front of the open window. All of the Bennets were standing there. "We are saved! Oh, I am the happiest mother alive! Wait until Lady Lucas hears this! Two daughters engaged! And Lizzy with the finest catch of all!" Mrs. Bennet twirled, and Mr. Bennet waltzed her away from the window.

Miss Hale called the youngest away. Miss Bennet smiled and pulled the curtains closed, offering them a measure of privacy (only a measure, for Darcy was certain he saw the curtains in the upstairs windows moving).

Elizabeth wrapped her arms around him, her fingers trailing up his back and tickling his neck when she twirled her fingers into his hair. "There is no gentleman in the world I could ever be prevailed upon to marry but you, Fitzwilliam."

Darcy knew he grinned like a fool, but he had never felt this happy before. He fairly burst with felicity.

Ruby licked his hand, and he looked down to see her sitting like a properly trained dog, the only sign of her excitement her tail chopping at the grass behind her. Darcy did not need to bend over any more to stroke her smooth fur. "Good girl," he said, raising his thumb for her to see before returning his attention fully to the woman in his arms. The woman who would be his wife. His Elizabeth.

He leaned forward, and she boldly rose to her toes, clutching the front of his shirt and pulling him closer and ruining the cravat Chalmers had so meticulously tied earlier that morning (not that he would mind when he learned that it was Elizabeth's doing).

The squeals at the window faded away, as did the rest of the world. His senses filled only with Elizabeth. She whispered, "I love you, Fitzwilliam," against his lips, making an already promising day absolutely perfect. Then he kissed her, and Darcy had to raise his concept of perfection.

CHAPTER 34

ONE MONTH LATER...

Chalmers stepped away, admiring his handiwork. Darcy inwardly grimaced at the ridiculous amount of folds cascading down his front, but since Elizabeth had praised Chalmers' exertions at their wedding the week before—the result of a weak moment his valet had expertly exploited—Darcy had had little say in the arrangement of his cravat.

"Thank you, Chalmers." Out of habit, he flipped his thumbs up, then folded his arms over his chest in an attempt to disguise the gesture. Chalmers was neither deaf nor a dog to be praised with hand signals.

He nodded at his mother's jewelry case resting on the bed. A suite of matching sapphires and rubies nestled between clusters of diamonds. A necklace, earrings, brooch, bracelet, ring, and tiara—a complete parure.

Elizabeth would look radiant. Darcy imagined her entering the ballroom looking like the Queen of Sheba. He wanted her first night, her debut into society as his wife, to leave a lasting memory on those in attendance. If they were going to talk, let them praise her beauty and bravery and of his pride in her. "Do you think Mrs. Darcy will approve of this selection?" he asked.

"Let us inquire to see Miss Ruby's opinion," Chalmers said. Leaning over Darcy's bed to gently tap on Ruby's shoulder, Chalmers pointed at the jewels with one hand while turning his thumb up with the other.

Ruby had wiggled her way into everyone's heart at Darcy House. Cook snuck her into the kitchen for bacon every morning, and Bates insisted on calling her Miss Ruby as though she were a proper lady. Even Chalmers had warmed to her.

Right now, Chalmers was speaking a language Ruby understood. The thumb up was her favorite gesture. Her deep *ruff* rumbled in the bedchamber. His expression devoid of all emotion, Chalmers said, "If Miss Ruby approves, then they are certain to be a favorite of Mrs. Darcy, sir. You two will be the handsomest couple at Lady Anglesey's ball."

Aunt Matlock had secured their invitations. The Countess of Anglesey's youngest daughter was out in society, her eldest son had finally married, and their mother insisted on ending the season with the largest, most extravagant ball to celebrate their family's successes.

It would be Darcy and Elizabeth's greatest test.

He had offered to have another gown specially made for her by the finest dressmaker in London, but Elizabeth had firmly refused, saying she would rather spend her first week as a married woman with her husband than spending hours getting fitted at the dressmaker's. Darcy had not argued the point—What new husband with an adorably captivating wife would? —but now he wondered if he should have insisted.

Still, he trusted Elizabeth to know her own mind. Therefore, instead of assuming she would allow him to drape her in jewels, he decided to consult with her first. Grabbing his mother's treasures along with the box of macarons Bingley had sent, he crossed the floor to the door connecting his room to Elizabeth's. It was usually open.

Ruby trotted alongside him, and he signaled for her to be quiet.

He knocked on Elizabeth's bedchamber door. No reply.

Gently, he nudged the barrier open and stepped inside. There was nobody, but he heard Georgiana's voice coming from the direction of the dressing room. "Are you not nervous at all? Everyone will be watching, inspecting and searching for flaws. I would be terrified!"

"Let them look!" Elizabeth said, laughter in her tone. "I daresay they have as many flaws as I do. Besides, with your brother at my side, how could I possibly be nervous?"

Darcy's pride inflated, then deflated like a popped balloon when his sister giggled. "He will glare them down, each and every one of them." She sighed. "Still, I am content to wait another year before I come out."

"And you will have both your brother and me to help you."

"And Jane!"

Georgiana had joined them in Hertfordshire for the reading of the banns and the double wedding. She had made quick friends of the Bennets, Miss Hale, and the youngest Lucas daughter, but she and Jane had connected like long-lost friends from the moment they first met.

Remembering what he held and why he was standing in the middle of his wife's bedchamber, Darcy signaled for Ruby to sit and then stepped forward to knock on the wall of the dressing room.

His breath caught in his throat at the vision twirling in front of the mirror. Elizabeth's hair was arranged with ringlets framing her face, making her eyes seem larger, more captivating. Wisps curled at the nape of her neck, that tender spot Darcy liked to nuzzle. She wore the same gown she had worn on their wedding day, a creamy silk with blue embroidery at the hem and sleeves—a perfect match for his mother's jewels. He crossed the room, loving how she naturally inclined her face toward him so he could kiss her on the cheek.

Running her fingers gently over his cravat, she grinned. "Chalmers is a master."

"He will be happy to hear your praise." Darcy handed the macarons to Georgiana. "Bingley sent these with a note wishing us well at our debut."

"You could read his writing?" Georgiana teased, plucking the ribbon off the container.

"Not at all. However, he had the good sense to marry a woman with an elegant and legible hand." He set the jewel case on the table and opened the lid.

Elizabeth pressed her fingers over her mouth. "They are stunning!"

Georgiana's hand hovered over her heart. "It is the set Mama wore for her portrait. It is my favorite painting at Pemberley."

Elizabeth spun to him. "You would dress me like a queen tonight!"

"I am proud of you and wish for you to feel every advantage."

She stepped closer to him, taking his hand and pressing his palm against her cheek. "Then dance with me tonight more than you should, stay at my side when the young men slip into the card room and the older gentlemen retire to the library. Let us sip champagne and talk and laugh like we are the only ones in the room."

"I will dance only with you."

She stepped away, dropping his hand. "You will do no such thing!"

Georgiana instantly took Elizabeth's side. "You must dance, Brother!"

"Furthermore," Elizabeth added, "you will ask the ladies sitting at the edge of the dance floor to stand with you, thus inspiring the other gentlemen to do the same and preventing their last ball of the season from being unmemorable. I shall look on in approval, and you shall do your best not to glare at my dance partner while I try not to look like I am counting down the seconds until we are in each other's immediate company again."

Already the thought of Elizabeth dancing with other men heated Darcy's blood. He did not know how he would manage—but manage he must.

She returned to the box of jewels and plucked out a bracelet. It was the simplest piece in the set. A simple ruby on a gold bangle. Slipping it over her dainty hand, she spun around and lifted the curls from her neck. "Will you help me with the clasp?" She nodded at the ruby necklace she always wore.

Darcy pretended a curl was in his way so he had an excuse to touch her silky hair. Then, he fumbled with the clasp so he could linger near her.

With a knowing smile, Elizabeth turned around to face him, looking over his shoulder. "Will this do, Miss Ruby?" she asked, signaling for Ruby to come. "You have an important job tonight, young miss, protecting

Georgiana and keeping her entertained while we are away." She pointed at her eyes and then at Georgiana, and Ruby sat on Georgie's feet as though she understood every word perfectly. She probably did. The George Wickhams of the world had no chance of getting near Georgiana with her giant sentinel watching over her.

"Are you certain you only wish to wear the bracelet? They are yours now, and you have every right to wear them," Darcy said.

She fingered the bracelet around her wrist. "Tonight, my aim is to convince everyone in attendance that we are deeply in love—that it is you and not your fortune which makes us happy."

"You make me happy."

"And I challenge you to show it this evening."

Darcy determined to dance every set, to laugh at every opportunity. It was true that he raised Elizabeth's status, but the truth of the matter was that she gave him much more than he could give her in return. She had unlocked within him an immeasurable joy and a newfound enthusiasm for life. Their legacy went beyond Pemberley and the wealth they would pass on to their children and grandchildren to something infinitely more valuable—love, happiness, and boundless promise.

They kissed and teased all the way to the ball which, fortunately for the state of their attire, was not far. Surely that was a sort of accomplishment—

kissing your wife without crushing her gown. It ought to be.

There was already a line to greet their hostess, and none other than Lady Jersey stood beside her. The ladies openly assessed Elizabeth from the moment they crossed the threshold into the entrance hall. By the time they reached Lady Anglesey, Darcy could hardly hear anything over the beating of his own heart.

"Mrs. Darcy, you have been the talk of London this past month." Her Ladyship looked Elizabeth over from top to bottom, her eyes narrowed.

Elizabeth smiled. "How dull for you, Lady Anglesey."

Lady Jersey interjected, "Scandal is rarely dull."

Lifting her chin with an impish grin, Elizabeth retorted, "If marrying for love is scandalous, then I shall shock your guests when I show a blatant preference for my husband's company. Or was that why you invited us, My Lady? If so, I applaud you, for Fitzwilliam and I are certain to provide enough conversation and 'scandal' to keep your guests entertained."

Lady Anglesey dismissed them and whispered into Lady Jersey's ear. "She will do."

Lady Jersey replied, "It is to her credit she did not arrive draped in Darcy jewels."

Darcy swore never to doubt Elizabeth's judgment again. He led her to the ballroom where they would face society's finest. "Are you ready, my love?"

She smiled up at him. "If I can win you over, then my odds are fair with them tonight."

He laughed aloud, earning him several glances. Let them look. If they saw how happy his wife made him, how delightful she was, then he would laugh all night—which he did—often enough for his aunt and all of her influential friends to notice.

A few hours later, Darcy heard Elizabeth's modest taste described as elegant, her conversation as witty. Aunt Matlock invited them to dine along with a few other select guests which (though Darcy did not admit to Elizabeth) had made his heart flip like a cart's wheel in his chest while he also groaned in impatience. Would the night never end? Would he never get Eliza beth to Pemberley?

Elizabeth knew this and no doubt felt similarly. When he had shown her the library at Darcy House, she was delighted. He could only imagine how she would react when she saw Pemberley's library.

After a particularly difficult dance where Darcy's partner lacked in grace but abounded in conversation, Elizabeth caught his eye, summoning him out to the balcony with a flicker of a glance. Seeing his talkative partner back to her chair, Darcy followed his wife, his relief great.

Elizabeth shivered, and Darcy wrapped his arms around her shoulders, pulling her closer to him. She snuggled against him with a satisfied sigh. "We shall have more invitations than we can accept if everyone makes good on their threats."

He chuckled. "I had hoped to depart for Pemberley before the week, but at this rate, it will be July or August before we can leave town." Right when the Thames was at its most repulsive peak.

"I have heard that the Thames is at its most rancid about then. Uncle Gardiner usually plans a tour of the countryside around then."

"I hope you will invite them to Pemberley."

"Where the library is grand and the air is pure?"

"And there are many conveniently placed gardens, groves, and alcoves where a man might kiss his wife without causing a scene."

She hummed a sigh, her breath tickling his neck and sending shivers through him.

"Darcy! There you are!" Richard sauntered over to them, interrupting their lovely flirtation. "The public is clamoring for her lively conversation."

Darcy tightened his grip around Elizabeth. "The public can wait."

"You cannot stay outside flirting with your wife."

His face brushed against Elizabeth's hair as he doubled over in laughter. A memory had surfaced at the perfect time to torment his cousin, and Darcy was in the mood to make good use of it. "I recall you swearing on your honor that the day you saw me flirting, you would flounce down the lane with an ostrich feather stuffed in your hat."

"You did not!" Elizabeth giggled. "Oh, I should love to see that!"

Richard did not share in their amusement. "I was speaking metaphorically."

Darcy retorted, "Lady Jersey has three ostrich feathers in her turban. I daresay she would be willing to spare one for the entertainment you would provide."

"It was a metaphor! Now are you two going to waste your humor on me or are you going to direct it where it will most benefit you?" Richard held out his arm, and Elizabeth cast Darcy a pouty look before she took it. Darcy wanted to pout, too.

Richard clucked his tongue and shook his head. "I expect you inside shortly too."

Darcy saluted at him, and Richard guffawed until Elizabeth asked him what his mother thought about Miss Hale.

Darcy watched them disappear into the crush. The one constant in his courtship with Elizabeth had been interruptions, and while he had lamented and cursed them at the time, they had also taught him a great deal. Enough to know that his education was only beginning.

He had once thought time was his greatest foe, preventing him from proposing until he was capable of being a better husband. But along with the other humbling realizations, his perception of time had also undergone a change. What had once been an enemy was now an ally.

Elizabeth was in his life, and they had all the time in the world.

~

When love needs a helping hand—or paw—these lovable critters come to Darcy and Elizabeth's rescue.
Read all the standalone books in the Love's Little Helpers series!

Visit jenniferjoywrites.com to see all Jennifer's books!

THANK YOU!

Thank you for reading *A Perfectly (Un)timely Proposal*! Of all the stories you could read, I'm honored you chose mine. I hope you enjoyed it, and I'd love to hear your thoughts in a review on Amazon and Goodreads! Want to know when my next book is available? Join my newsletter for regular updates, sales, bonus scenes, and your free novelette!

ABOUT THE AUTHOR

When Jennifer isn't busy dreaming up new adventures for her favorite characters, she is learning Sign language, reading, baking (Cake is her one weakness!), or chasing her twins around the park (because ... cake).

She believes in happy endings, sweet romance, and plenty of mystery. She also believes there's enough angst on the news, so she keeps her stories light-hearted and full of hope.

While she claims Oregon as her home, she currently lives high in the Andes Mountains of Ecuador with her husband and two kids.

Connect with Jennifer!
jenniferjoywrites.com

Made in the USA
Coppell, TX
05 December 2022